The Intergenerational Church

Understanding Congregations from WWII to www.com

Peter Menconi

Mt. Sage Publishing
Littleton, CO

Published by Mt. Sage Publishing
P.O. Box 2209
Littleton, CO 80161-2209
www.msagepublishing.com

First edition published 2008.
Printed in the United States of America.

ISBN: 1-4537-3470-8
ISBN-13: 9781453734704

Contents

Preface

It happened rather unexpectedly. I had read Strauss and Howe's book *Generations* some years before and was interested in how different generations related in our church. I decided to preach a two-part series on the inter-generational church expressing why I thought the different generations were better together. The first Sunday I asked five people from different generations to speak for five minutes while answering three questions: 1. What events have shaped your generation? 2. How does God speak to your generation? 3. What does your generation have to offer to the kingdom of God? Needless to say, this was a formidable task. Each of the people did very well in succinctly and powerfully answering the questions.

The first unexpected occurrence was visual. The member of the GI Generation, a World War II vet, wore a coat, tie, and vest. The Silent Generation representative wore a sport coat with a turtleneck shirt. The woman who spoke for the Boomer Generation wore casual business clothes. The Gen Xer wore khaki pants and an informal short-sleeved shirt. And the Millennial college student wore a tee shirt, baggy pants, and boots. As the generational representatives got younger, the clothes got more casual.

As each of the age group spokespersons answered the questions, the major characteristics of each generation began to unfold. The Gler spoke of the hardships when growing up in the Midwest during the Great Depression. He was an only child because his parents could not afford others. He told how his small farming community banded together to help each other survive this difficult time. The Gler revealed that as a young man he entered the military to serve his country because that was what young men did in his day. After seeing combat in the Pacific theater, he returned to attend college on the GI Bill. He shared that his life was completely changed when he received a college education through the GI Bill. After college the Gler went on to own several successful businesses and today continues to contribute to God's kingdom as he moves through his eighties.

The representative of the Silent Generation was a retired university administrator who spoke of having it easy in comparison to the GIs. He felt that his coming-of-age years were quite trouble free and actually described his generation as growing up in la-la land. The Silent Generation spokesperson depicted his generation as hardworking and compliant. While his generation was made up of good folks, there was little outstanding or distinctive about his peer group.

The woman who represented the Boomer Generation was the executive director of a nonprofit with a national influence. She talked passionately about her generation's desire to change the world. Having lived through tremendous social upheaval and change, she felt Boomers were still the best equipped to lead the process of constructive social transformation. From her presentation it was apparent that

Boomers were not planning on fading into the sunset anytime soon.

The Gen Xer started his talk questioning if he was, in fact, a member of Generation X. So he googled the term "Gen X" and discovered that he fit the description of this generation quite well. He came from a home where his parents had divorced; he took quite a while to make a career decision; he embraced a laidback live-and-let-live philosophy of life. As he spoke, tentativeness and uncertainty about life was communicated.

The Millennial Generation was represented by a college student who spoke with self-assurance and confidence. He talked of the great impact technology, globalization, and postmodernism was having on his generation. He expressed the belief that his generation would be up for the challenges that faced them. Perhaps it was youthful optimism, but he clearly expressed the positive confidence that is present in many Millennials.

In the span of less than an hour our congregation experienced another unexpected reality—the remarkable diversity that existed in our church. No one could have left that service believing that all generations today see the world in the same way. It would take people a while to process what they had seen and heard.

A week later in the second sermon I presented an overview of the five generations in our church community. Specifically, we looked at the life events and values that shaped each generation and the responses of each age group to popular culture, church, and spirituality. I offered practical ways for the different generations to relate beyond superficial levels. In short, the congregation was stirred to consider that despite our differences, we are better together.

After the service and for months to follow I received comments such as, "Now I understand my children better" or "Now I appreciate my parents more." The frequency and intensity of the feedback helped me to realize that I had stumbled over something important. Consequently, over the past several years I have been researching, discussing, speaking on, and writing about the importance of churches becoming intergenerational. This book is the result of this activity. I believe the pages that follow will launch you on your own intergenerational journey—in your family, with your friends, in your workplace, and in your church.

As is quite apparent, a book is not written without help from many. I want to thank many friends who have read the manuscript and given me invaluable comments and insights. This book is better because of your investment. Most of all, I would like to thank my wife, Jean, for her patience and loving support through the many obstacles and complexities of bringing this book to completion.

My hope and prayer is that this book will become a valuable catalyst in helping you and your church become exceedingly more effective in ministering intergenerationally for God and his kingdom.

Peter Menconi
January, 2010

Introduction

Churches at Risk

Jim has been the pastor of The First Community Church for nine years and now he is starting to feel uneasy. When he took over from the founding pastor he had to work hard to make changes in the way the church ministered. He grew the church over the years but now notices that attendance is slowly dropping. Jim also observes that he is preaching to a sea of graying heads. "How has the congregation aged so quickly? Where are the young people?" He uncomfortably realizes that his church is slowly dying and without an influx of younger people, it will be retired when he does. While there are plenty of young singles, couples, and families moving into the community, few return to his church after their first visit or two. Jim spends many sleepless nights mulling over the question, "How do I get younger people to come, stay, and become active participants in ministry." Clearly, First Community is a church at risk. Sound familiar?

If we take an honest look at churches today, we realize that most churches in America have either reached a plateau or are in decline. Even most of the churches that are growing are increasing through transfer growth or church switching. A brief summary of church attendance statistics give us a better picture of today's churches:

- The percentage of people attending a Christian church on any weekend is far below what pollsters report. (see www.theamericanchurch.org)
- Weekend attendance at Christian churches has stayed virtually the same since 1990. (see www.theamericanchurch.org)
- Millennials are least likely to attend church in a typical weekend (33%), followed by Gen X (43%), then Boomers (49%), and finally Silents and GIs (54%). (see www.barna.org)
- Established churches are declining in attendance by 1-2 percent per year. (see www.theamericanchurch.org)
- More than two-thirds of young adults who attend a Protestant church in high school will drop out of church for at least a year before their 22nd birthday. (see www.lifeway.com)

According to a recent survey conducted by LifeWay Research (see www.lifeway.com), many young adults are leaving churches or do not attend because they find it irrelevant to their lives. While many young adults seek community and relationships with others, they indicate that the lack of opportunities for connection within the church is frustrating and discouraging. If churches are to attract young adults, they must make room for them. Since young people see the world differently, keeping them involved will form a major challenge for most churches.

Many church leaders do not understand that generational differences and misunderstandings put their churches at risk. Without healthy intergenerational interaction most churches will become isolated and marginalized. On the surface relationships between generations in your church may seem to be going well. A deeper look offers a different picture. While many churches are *multigenerational* and seemingly healthy on the surface, in reality, the generations act like ships in the night that pass by one another but rarely have meaningful contact and interaction. This lack of significant communication and relations between generations must be addressed if churches are to thrive—not merely survive—now and in the future.

Pause for a moment the next time you stop for a cup of coffee at the local mall or walk through an airport. Take a look around. How many different generations do you see? As you move through your day, pay attention to the different age groups you interact with in your home, community, school, and workplace. Chances are good that you casually interact with at least three or more different generations each day. For example, the young man who waited on you at Starbucks may be a Millennial or Gen Xer. At work, you may find yourself interacting and cooperating (or not cooperating) with members of several generations. Everyday, members of different generations bump up against each other, but rarely do they really understand one another. This same lack of insight between generations exists in our churches. This book will help you understand and appreciate today's generations and learn how they can be united into a healthy, vital, and effective intergenerational church.

Generational Generalities

As we look at the various age groups, generalities on each generation will be made. The words *generation* and *generality* come from the same root word that means "to bring forth." A closer look at our current generations *brings forth* certain generalities. These generalities do not fit all members of a generation, but they are representative of the majority of people in any given age group. Before you discount statements about your generation or another, please read on.

People who are born within a few years of the end or beginning of a generation are *cuspers* and may show characteristics of two generations. In the following example, one cusper may show the behaviors of the Silent Generation while another cusper of the same age may take on the behaviors of the Boomer Generation. The diagram below shows how generational generalities impact the majority of members in a given generation:

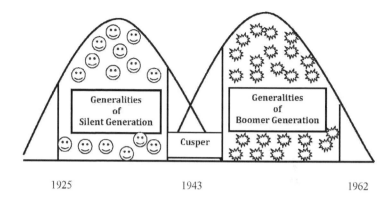

1925   1943   1962

Cuspers often blur the lines between generations. For example, Bob Dylan and Joan Baez (both born in 1941) and the late Jimi Hendrix and Jerry Garcia (both born in 1942) are technically members of the Silent Generation, yet these cuspers are closely identified with the Boomer Generation.

Generational behavior is affected by a number of factors. The following are just some of the elements that can influence behavior within a generation:

- *Location and regionalism:* Where you grow up is significant. The life experiences created by urban, suburban, and rural lifestyles can differ enough to affect one's worldview. Also, different regions of the United States produce nuances in people's behavior. For example, a Boomer coming of age in the 1960s in Ottumwa, Iowa would probably have different experiences and a different worldview than a same-aged Boomer growing up in Berkeley, California. As the world becomes increasingly globalized, more and more regional (and even national) differences are disappearing, or at least being diluted.

- **Socioeconomic:** Whether you are rich, middle class, or poor will also impact your behavior. More financial resources usually mean more options. With money, for example, you can travel and see the world. The poor rarely have the opportunity to leave their own city or town, let alone their country, to see how others live and think.

- **Ethnicity and race:** Your race and ethnicity can produce subtle differences. Most African-Americans see the world very differently from most Anglos, Latinos, and Asian-Americans, and vice versa. Despite these differences, diverse peoples of the same generations often embrace similar worldviews.

- **Education:** Different educational levels within a generation also will produce some divergence in lifestyle perspectives and behaviors.

Even with these factors, the generalities within a generation are remarkably consistent.

The Six Generations

To begin the process of uniting our generations into the diverse body and church God intended, we need to understand the different generations. Perhaps you are not familiar with the different generations that darken (or fail to darken) the doors of your church. Currently, there is the possibility of six generations attending a church's worship service and ministry activities each week. It is generally accepted that a new generation starts about every seventeen to twenty years. Consequently, these six generations span almost a hundred years of the most phenomenal changes in human history. It is a group that has literally gone from WWI and WWII to www.com. Given this reality, it is not surprising that many American churches are experiencing a breakdown in communication between the generations.

Both in the popular media and in academia there has been much discussion on the dates and names of each generation. As there is no consensus on the naming of generations or the specific time frame of their run, the generational names and dates used in this book represent a compromise of numerous authoritative and popular sources. The following summary provides a brief description of each generation:

> **GI Generation:** Born between 1906 and 1924, this generation has been labeled *The Greatest Generation* by Tom Brokaw and others. They have also been called the Heroic Generation and Civic Generation because they were the primary age group to suffer through the Great Depression and win World War II.

> **Silent Generation:** Born between 1925 and 1943, this generation also has been called the Builder, the Beat, the Beatnik, the Radio, and the Peacemaker Generation.

> **Boomer Generation:** Born between 1944 and 1962, this generation also has been labeled the Baby Boom, the Hippie, the Yippie, the TV, the Flower Children, the Me Generation and more.

Generation X: Born between 1963 and 1981, this generation is also known as Gen X, the Baby Busters, the 13th Generation, the Computer Generation, the .com Generation and more.

Millennial Generation: Born between 1982 and 2000, this generation also is called Generation Y, Generation Why?, the Always-On Generation, Generation D (for "digital"), Generation Text, the Bridger Generation, and more.

Generation Z(?): This new, unnamed generation started with those born in 2001.

Generations	Years Born
GI Generation	1906 to 1924
Silent Generation	1925 to 1943
Boomer Generation	1944 to 1962
Generation X	1963 to 1981
Millennial Generation	1982 to 2000
Generation Z (?)	2001 +

While members of all these generations may be in your church today, we will concentrate on the GIs, Silents, Boomers, Gen Xers and Millennials in this book.

Part 1
Intergenerational Realities

Chapter 1
Why Intergenerational Ministry?

America and American churches are experiencing a quiet but profound transformation. For the first time in human history five (with the ongoing addition of a sixth) generations are living side by side. How these generations relate to each other over the next years and decades will determine the course of America and American churches. Over the next several decades, intergenerational churches have great potential to impact individual lives and transform society. The degree to which churches are successful in achieving effective intergenerational ministry will determine the effectiveness of their overall ministries.

Churches with one dominant generation, no matter what generation it is, are most at risk for ineffectual ministry. While churches with two dominant generations are somewhat more effective, they generally fall quite short of their ministry potential. Multigenerational churches, which have several generations attending but few meaningful, growing relationships between the different generations, will be even more effective in ministry, but will be less effective than intergenerational churches. By contrast, intergenerational churches experience many healthy relationships between the different generations that lead to effective ministry. Effective intergenerational ministry allows all age groups to feel at home as they participate in the life of the church.

Generations at Risk

As life expectancy in the United States continues to grow and as birthrates increase, churches are faced with the reality that multiple generations are worshipping under the same roof. The coexistence of numerous generations in the same church is often not a *peaceful* coexistence. Too often individual generations are vying and competing for church time, space, and resources. In churches where one generation controls the power, other generations are relegated to second-class citizenship or even driven out of the church. For example, a powerful director of the children's program (who has held the position for fifteen years) may want a series of bulletin boards in the same space that the upstart young adults group sees as a wonderful art gallery. Who usually wins this competition? Another typical confrontation between generations in the church arises over the type and style of music used in a worship service. Rather than reaching for intergenerational solutions, *worship wars* often end with one generation winning and another losing.

It is interesting that few churches are aware of these generational problems, let alone addressing them. Usually churches and church leadership believe that younger generations must wait their turn and pay their dues before they can help shape a church's ministry and future. Churches that take this approach are at risk of losing a generation or two from their congregation. Many will find themselves as predominately *mono-generational* churches. The challenges of becoming and sustaining intergenerational churches are with us—they will not be going away soon.

The obvious first step in moving toward intergenerational ministry is to acknowledge that your church can and must do a better job of creating healthy intergenerational relationships and developing an effective intergenerational philosophy and ministry. A second step in this process is to understand the importance of a healthy intergenerational ministry. Here are a few reasons why intergenerational ministry is so critical—you may want to add some of your own:

- **All generations are important to God.** (Even a cursory word study of *generations* in the Bible will reveal this point.)
- **We need to understand and honor those who have gone before us.**
- **We need to intentionally think about and act on leaving a Christ-centered legacy for future generations.**
- **A healthy intergenerational church is a powerful witness to our secular society.**
- **We need to understand other current generations so that we can learn from them, and them from us.** A local church will be much healthier (spiritually and relationally) if its younger members learn from its older members and vice versa.
- **Future leaders will develop more easily in an intergenerational church.**

- **A church that does not understand and respond to changing times quickly grows stale and irrelevant.**
- **Everyone in the church, no matter what age they are, has something to offer God.** If we fail to give everyone an opportunity to minister, we waste the resources of God's kingdom.
- **God, through Scripture, has instructed the church to be a unified body in the midst of tremendous diversity—that diversity extends to generational diversity.**

Generations in the Bible

When the words *generation* or *generations* appear in the Bible, they usually have one of two distinct meanings. First, it may refer to a group of people who live or lived during the same period of history. In Deuteronomy 32:5, for example, Moses chides his generation saying, "They have acted corruptly toward him (God); to their shame they are no longer his children, but a warped and crooked generation." Second, the term *generation* may refer to a group of individuals who share common ancestry. In this sense, a *generation* represents a genealogy or family tree.

God has always considered generations and intergenerational relationships to be important. From the beginning, God has connected and ministered to generations. In Genesis 17, God tells Abram that he will make him the father of many nations. In verse 7 we read, "I will establish my covenant as an everlasting covenant between me and you and your descendants after you for the generations to come, to be your God and the God of your descendants after you." The genealogy of Jesus in the gospels of Matthew and Luke gives his earthly life a context in God's history. In less dramatic and critical ways, our generations give each of us a sense of time and place in God's history.

I was recently reminded of my own spiritual heritage when the 100th year anniversary of the beginning of my grandfather's ministry was celebrated. (Perhaps this centennial is especially poignant because I was named after him.) He was born in Italy in 1873 and immigrated to Chicago in 1890. There he became a candy maker, married, and fathered 13 children. Raised a Roman Catholic, he accepted Jesus Christ as his Savior and Lord in 1900 and became a Presbyterian. In the wake of the Azusa Street Revival in Los Angeles, my grandfather received the baptism of the Holy Spirit. In 1907 he began to pastor a Pentecostal church while working full-time as a candy maker. Numerous Italian-American churches sprang from his original church and many continue ministering to this day.

In his wake my grandfather left a spiritual legacy that lived and lives on in subsequent generations. Numerous family members are involved in a variety of ministries and churches all over the country. In our fast paced world, we rarely stop to reflect upon the generations that have come before. Their influences on our lives, both positive and negative, need to be understood and appreciated.

In addition to honoring the past, we are to look to future generations and take some responsibility for them. In Psalms 22, a Messianic psalm, we read in verses 30 and 31 that "Posterity will serve him; future generations will be told about the Lord. They will proclaim his righteousness to a people yet unborn—for he has done it." It is quite apparent that we have the responsibility to teach, direct, and train younger generations. For instance, the psalmists writes, "Even when I am old and gray, do not forsake me, O God, till I declare your power to the next generation, your might to all who are to come" (Psalms 71:18).

Understanding and Honoring the Past

American writer Robert Heinlein wrote that "A generation which ignores history has no past and no future." The Bible is certainly a book of the past, present, and future. It tells us that to understand the present, we must learn from the past. Certainly, while we do not want to dwell in and on the past, we ignore it at our own peril. Understanding and appreciating the history of those who have come before us is a great way for us to understand our present and gain insight for our future. A healthy intergenerational church appreciates and learns from its past but does not necessarily replicate it in the present or in the future.

A Church for All Generations

Is your church a church for all of today's generations? With the forces of change buffeting churches today, we need the wisdom of all generations to guide us into the future. Unfortunately, most churches have leadership from only one or two generations. No matter which generations they represent, leaders from one or two generations cannot understand or respond to the various needs of our generationally diverse culture. Consequently, many churches are quickly becoming irrelevant in a multigenerational society.

Many members of the younger generations find it difficult to relate to church as it is "done" by older generations.

In fact, many young people have stopped trying to find God in most of our churches. They find it difficult to get beyond the styles of worship or church politics. One response young people have for this dilemma is to start churches that meet their generation's needs. These mono-generational churches incorporate music and worship styles that appeal to younger people. But single generation churches are not the answer to our multigenerational spiritual needs. In fact, many newer generationally based churches have begun to rethink and modify their ministries as they discover limitations in ministering primarily to one generation.

Despite all the difficulties inherent in establishing an intergenerational church, it is very much worth the effort. Consider that the local church is one of the last places in our society where all the generations can come together in a meaningful way. The metaphor for the church in scripture is that of a *body* where diverse parts interdependently work together. That is, with Jesus Christ as the head, other parts of the body (the hand, arm, feet, eyes, etc.) are to cooperate and collaborate together to further God's kingdom here on earth. The different generations in the church represent some of these diverse body parts. Consequently, a healthy church will find creative ways to involve all its generations and engage them in significant ways.

Choosing Change

It has become cliché to talk about the rapid pace of change in our society and world. Whether cliché or not, rapid change is with us, and it is not going away. Churches are not immune to the changes taking place in our society.

Peter Menconi

The following are some of the major developments in our society to which churches must respond:

- ***A multigenerational change in the population distribution***: America's population is aging. Instead of a pyramidal distribution with younger generations at the bottom, our population is headed toward a population distribution that looks more like a column. That is, the number of people in our society's various age groups is becoming more equal. Roughly speaking, the change in the U.S. population distribution from 1900 to 2030 will look something like this:

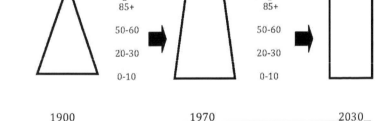

The reality is that we are on the verge of a major generational shift in many churches, especially in mainline denominations. A church that has intentionally become intergenerational has already dealt with significant change and is better prepared to keep responding to change. The local church that has intentionally become intergenerational has chosen to change and views change as a necessary part of a more effective ministry. The fresh flow of ideas and interaction between and within generations helps the intergenerational church maintain its vitality. Remember that everyone, no matter what their age, has something to offer God and his kingdom.

- ***A multicultural, multiethnic, multireligious society:*** New census results revealed the reality of a new America: America has become a mosaic of people from many nations with various cultures who practice different, even strange, religions. Immigrants from Latin America, Asia, and Africa are increasing while the percentage of Americans with European roots is decreasing. For example, New Mexico and Hawaii are states where all ethnic and racial groups are already in the minority. Demographers predict that by 2060, all ethnic and racial groups in America will be in the minority, even Anglos. That is, no ethnic or racial group will represent over fifty percent of the population. In reality, by 2060, ethnicity and race may lose much of today's meaning and the term *minority* will become pointless.

Legal and illegal migration from south of the border has made Latinos the largest minority group in the United States. While southern and western states in particular have experienced this influx of Latino peoples and cultures, large numbers of immigrants from Mexico and Central America can be found in every state. In fact, there are numerous places in America where Spanish is a primary—if not *the* primary—language of communication. In the cities of Miami and San Antonio, the majority of the population is Latino. Even the midwestern city of Chicago has a population makeup of nearly 20 percent Latino.

New census data also show that immigrants from Asia have come to the United States in record numbers and have settled mainly in West Coast states. As with Latino communities, there are many Asian neighborhoods where English is not the primary language spoken. Additionally, Latino and Asian families tend to have more children, resulting in a high percentage of their population being under the age of twenty five.

America's large African-American population can be added to this complex mosaic. Increasingly, immigrant populations are replacing traditional black communities in many cities. In response, many African-American families are relocating from urban centers to older, "first-ring" suburbs. The landscape of America is changing. How will our churches respond?

- ***Families are increasingly diverse:*** Families today are a far cry from the two-parent, one-income families of classic TV's Nelsons and Cleavers. Now a "family" is defined in a number of different ways. In addition to two-parent families, we have single-parent families, blended families with at least one stepparent, grandparent-led families, same-sex parent families, multiracial families, adoptive families, and intergenerational families. No longer can there be a one-size-fits-all ministry to families.

Interestingly, numerous surveys hint that the family may be making a comeback. That is, parents today seem to be placing a greater importance on their children and family life than did parents in the previous two or three decades. And despite the differences in family types today, many things about families remain the same. Parents still love their children. Family members still love and care for each other, still look out for each other, especially during difficult times. Again, an intergenerational church is better equipped to minister to the wide variety of families in our society.

- **The world is becoming "smaller" through globalization:** While there are various definitions for the word *globalization*, in its simplest form it means *the emergence of a worldwide perspective in many areas of human activity.* For instance, we can talk of the globalization of the economy, the globalization of culture, the globalization of politics, the globalization of communication, and so on. The following anonymous e-mail message making the rounds gives us a humorous, if irreverent, definition of globalization:

Question: *What is the truest definition of "Globalization?"*
Answer: *Princess Diana's death.*
Question: *How come?*
Answer: *An English princess with an Egyptian boyfriend crashes in a French tunnel, driving a German car with a Dutch engine, driven by a Belgian who was drunk on Scottish whisky, (check the bottle before you change the spelling) followed closely by Italian Paparazzi, on Japanese motorcycles; treated by an American doctor, using Brazilian medicines.*

This is sent to you by an American, using Bill Gates technology, and you're probably reading this on your computer, that uses Taiwanese chips, and a Korean monitor, assembled by Bangladeshi workers in a Singapore plant, transported by Indian lorry-drivers, hijacked by Indonesians, unloaded by Sicilian longshoremen, and trucked to you by Mexican illegals—
That, my friend, is Globalization!!

The impact of globalization is difficult to avoid—even if you want to.

It is to this globalized world that Jesus Christ has called his church to ministry. And in order for his church to be effective today, we must think globally as well as locally. The first step in engaging our changing world is to reorient our thinking. That is, we must begin to see our lives as taking place within a global context and system. American and Western churches no longer represent the center of God's activities on earth, if they ever did. In fact, about 70 percent of the Christians in the world live outside the West. Yet, most ministry resources are found in Western countries. Increasingly, the church in the West will be forced to change its business-as-usual attitude, if it is to be a major participant in worldwide ministry. Younger generations can bring a global perspective to the intergenerational church and will help it to respond more effectively to new global realities.

· ***Postmodernity will force our churches to minister differently:*** In recent years, much has been written about our current transition into a postmodern world. While postmodernism is still being defined and understood, it is clear that our society is going through a major shift in the way we look at the world. (More will be written about postmodernism later.) Consequently, traditional perspectives do not play well with many young adults. Business-as-usual theology and practice in our churches do not engage those who see our postmodern world as chaotic and relative. New and fresh ways of communicating timeless biblical realities and truths must be identified.

This needed change cannot be addressed by simply creating a *contemporary* or *emergent* service in a traditional church. It takes thoughtful reassessment and reevaluation of why and how we follow Jesus Christ. We need to strip away much of the baggage given to us by our modern perspectives of God, the Bible, and our culture. We will also find it instructive and constructive to reexamine what it means to have a relationship with Jesus Christ within premodern and postmodern worldviews. Most members of younger generations have postmodern perspectives. Churches need younger leaders to provide input that helps all of us to be more effective in connecting the Good News of Jesus Christ with this changing society.

With postmodernity, we meet fewer people in our society familiar with church culture. Many non-attendees see the church as a place for church people, but certainly not for them. Increasingly, there is a wider gap between the average church attendee and those who never or rarely attend a church. Consequently, Christians and non-Christians often do not speak the same cultural language and thus rarely connect in meaningful ways.

Unfortunately, when faced with these many changes, most church leaders respond poorly. Often a leader's response to the challenge of doing ministry differently will emanate from his or her generational experience and bias. It is not uncommon to hear the retort, "Why change? This is the way we have always done it." By contrast, leaders in intergenerational churches are regularly grappling with change and are better at handling it both inside and outside the church. A healthy intergenerational church that deals well with change can be a powerful witness to a searching culture. Our society has few places left where all generations can interact and grow together. If a local church is a place where people engage the issues and events of real life, it will be noticed. In fact, healthy intergenerational churches will not only be noticed, but new people will want to look, and come, closer.

Living an Eternal Legacy

If none of the preceding reasons for an intergenerational church convince you, think about this: We are instructed in scripture to develop and leave an eternal legacy. As we age, we often reflect on what kind of legacy we will leave—how will we be remembered? Do not wait until the end of your life to think and act on your legacy. Everyone, of any age, should reflect on the legacy that he or she is building. Jesus taught us in Matthew 7:24, 25 that "Everyone who hears these words of mine and puts them into practice is like a wise man who built his house on the rock. The rain came down, the streams rose, and the winds blew and beat against that house; yet it did not fall, because it had its foundation on the rock." Building our lives on our relationship with Jesus Christ and living our lives as his followers is our legacy as Christians. As we follow Jesus, our lives should be a living legacy for all generations around us, especially the younger ones. An intergenerational church will give us real and realistic opportunities to guide and mentor new generations and to leave a lasting legacy—a legacy for all eternity.

Peter Menconi

As you move toward becoming an intergenerational church, it is important that you assess and understand your current church population. The next chapter is designed to accomplish this. Subsequent chapters will address developing a philosophy of intergenerational ministry and understanding the generations in your church. These topics must be addressed and understood before your church can effectively develop a healthy intergenerational ministry.

The *Chapter 1 Worksheet* at the end of the book will assist you in assessing how well you understand intergenerational ministry. It will also help your church leadership assess how committed you are to becoming more intergenerational.

Chapter 2
Know Your Church: Who Are You, Really?

How well do you know and understand the generational makeup of your church? This question is not as easy to answer as you may think. Before you do a head count or express your personal judgment, have your church leadership give their generational assessment of your congregation. That is, have them take an educated guess on what percentage of your members and regular attendees fall into each generation or age group. (If necessary, review the generational categories found in the introduction.) Make this a fun exercise. For example, you may want to divide your leaders into several small groups and have each take their best guess. Later, when you have a more accurate accounting, see which group had the best guess. However you do it, a best-guess exercise will focus your leaders attention and observation skills on generational matters and prepare the way for the discussions and changes to follow.

Learn About Your People

After this initial estimation, start a more accurate assessment. If you have an up-to-date database of your congregation, this assessment is relatively easy. First, determine how many people and what percentage of your congregation are under twenty years of age; what number and percentage between twenty and forty; between forty-one and sixty; between sixty-one and seventy-five; and more than seventy-five years of age. If you do not have a readily available database of information on church members and attendees, there are a couple of things you can do to generate this data. One option is to create a survey distributed to all members and regular attendees (see sample survey in Chapter 2-Worksheet in the back of this book). Depending on the size of your church, you may get either a complete generational assessment or a representative sample from the returned surveys. It is usually best to get your congregation to fill out a survey before or after your worship times. (Once the surveys leave the building, you will get far less of them returned.) Another option is to have your leadership conduct a telephone survey. Direct contact with your congregation is almost always valuable. A telephone survey allows your leadership team the opportunity to explain your church's concern about the need for greater intergenerational contact and ministry. Whatever method of gathering information you use, the information will be invaluable in creating a new database with important demographics about your congregation.

While you will want to customize your survey to your congregation, the following are some of the questions you want answers to:

- *Into what generational age groups do our people fall? How many generations are represented in each of the families?*

- *From where are our people coming? How many drive more than two miles to attend our church? More than five miles? More than ten miles?*
- *If most commute from significant distances, why do they?*
- *Why do our people come to our church and not another? Are they drawn by denominational affiliation? Are they drawn by the preaching or worship style? Are they drawn by the community life of our church? Do the children's or youth programs interest them? Do the missions or outreach programs draw them?*
- *What is the general education level of our church? Are our people primarily high school graduates? College graduates or beyond?*
- *What is the general socioeconomic makeup of our congregation? What is the ethnic makeup of our church? Is it relatively homogeneous or is it quite diverse?*
- *What are the networks or spheres of influence within which our people are involved?*

Certainly, there are other questions you may want to ask, especially if your community has some unique characteristics. Make sure your congregation understands that this information is being collected so the church can minister to and through them more effectively. Also, let them know that the information collected will be held in confidence by the church leadership. In fact, the survey responses should be submitted anonymously.

Peter Menconi

Interpreting the Data

After you have gathered and calculated the generational data, it might be helpful to graph the results. For visually oriented people it is often easier to understand the results when presented graphically. The following graph is an example of a 250-attendee church and how its congregation might look as a young church, a middle-aged church, an aging church, or an aged church:

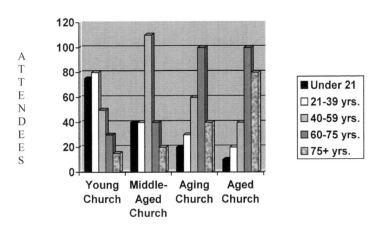

The next step in the assessment process is for the church leadership to discuss the results. Start by comparing the survey results with the educated guesses of your leadership team. Are there any surprises? Continue the discussion by asking the following questions, keeping the discussion going until your leaders gain some new insights into your congregation:

- *Are any of the presurvey guesses considerably different from the actual results? If so, why this discrepancy?*

- *Which generations are represented the most in our church? Which the least?*
- *Is one age group over represented? Why?*
- *How does the generational breakdown of our church compare with the generational breakdown of our community? Do we know the generational breakdown of our community?* (If not, some research is in order. Many demographic databases are available from your local government, library, and other resources.)
- *Do we (church leadership) have any desire to change the generational makeup of our church? If not, why not? If so, why?*
- *How might our church go about attracting larger numbers of the poorly attending generations?*

These questions should be enough to get a dialogue started. But talking about the generational makeup of your church is only the beginning. Don't get bogged down in the discussion. If you do, you will never get to your destination—becoming an effective intergenerational church.

A head count is only the first step in the generational assessment of your congregation. You can use the survey process as an opportunity to learn more about the people who cross the thresholds of your church each week. And do not limit your assessment only to people who attend your worship services. Your church has an impact on many other people throughout the week. As you begin to develop a generational strategy of ministry you may want to include some of the groups that use your facilities throughout the week. They may provide some valuable networking opportunities that will assist you in the development of your in-

Peter Menconi

tergenerational ministry. For example, a program for mothers of preschool children or an on-site preschool may form the basis for a mother's mentoring program where older mothers mentor and support younger mothers.

As you gather information about your attendees, ask them what they desire to get out of their church experience. That is, ask your people *why* they come to church. Here are some common responses:

- "I've attended church all my life—it's a habit."
- "I want to know God better."
- "I come to worship God."
- "I want to meet other people."
- "I desire to learn what the Bible says."
- "I'm curious about God's will for my life."
- "I would like to serve God and others."
- "I'm looking for answers to my problems."
- "I come because I'm desperate."
- "I want to find a mate."
- "I desire to expose my kids to moral and ethical teachings."
- "I want to get into heaven."
- "I come because my friends are here."
- "I am looking to grow spiritually."
- "I want to help change the world."
- "I would like to find peace."

These are some of the reasons why people attend your church. Which ones predominate in your congregation?

Different generations will have different reasons for attending your church—or for staying away. Older generations often attend church because they always have or because they believe in and join organizations. Younger generations are more independent and less inclined to attend and join churches. They often believe that their spiritual needs can be met elsewhere. Younger generations also believe they have other options and avenues in which to find and pursue God. (These differences between generations will be developed later in the book.)

Know Your Generational Philosophy

When it comes to the various generations in your church, what is your philosophy of ministry? Unfortunately, most pastors and church leaders cannot coherently answer this question. If any church is going to successfully navigate the transition into becoming an intergenerational church, it must have a philosophy of ministry that works. Consider the following generationally based ministry philosophies and identify one that best describes your church.

Dominant-Generation Ministry Philosophy

Churches that have a dominant-generation philosophy usually have a majority of attendees from one generation. This type of church takes on the popular cultural context, characteristics, and worldview of the dominant generation, no matter which generation it is. Consequently, a GI Generation-dominated church would most likely have a traditional worship service with an organ and choir. Sunday school classes usually take a didactic approach to the Bible. Church leadership places importance on an organization that is run well. The pastor is often viewed as a hired gun that preaches sermons, marries and buries, and provides pastoral care for the members.

A Silent Generation-dominated church will usually have similar characteristics with more variety in their Sunday school options. While this generation may place less emphasis on church polity, the church as an organization is still quite important. Also, the Silents respect people with credentials and those who get things done. Consequently, they expect the pastor to be a professional. To this generation, the church is an important place to develop social relationships. The Silent Generation also believes it is important that people in the church get along. While serving others is encouraged in the Silent-dominated church, little creative social action ministry will emerge.

A Boomer Generation-dominated church usually has a more contemporary worship service format. This generation is not very interested in Sunday school classes unless they present practical, useful information. Any small group experience for the Boomers cannot feature a talking head—they need interaction and participation. The Boomer-dominated church often provides a wide variety of services and opportunities that can be consumed by Boomers and their families. To Boomers, the church as an organization is only important if it offers relationship-building and networking opportunities, as well as usable services.

A Generation X-dominated church typically places high value on authentic worship. The church as an organization is relatively unimportant to this generation. Rather, Gen Xers want a church that offers opportunities for adventurous, exciting outreach and service. The use of technological bells and whistles is also important to this generation. Often a Gen X-dominated church is designed to meet the needs of singles and young couples. More recently, Gen

X-dominated churches are working hard to learn how to minister to couples with young children.

Churches dominated by the Millennial Generation are just beginning to develop. Early indications show that Millennial-dominated churches are quite serious about their journey with Jesus. Initial involvements find them in ministries oriented toward problem solving, such as responding to the AIDS crisis, homeless orphans, global exploitation of children, etc. As the world becomes more dangerous, Millennials may also look to their churches for comfort and answers. Millennials will probably be more comfortable in an intergenerational church than are Gen Xers.

Family-Based Ministry Philosophy

A church with a family-based philosophy of ministry usually serves two generations: parents and their children. Churches with a true family-based philosophy are not very common. In these churches, all ministries are designed with families in mind. The pastor usually gives a children's sermon or talk along with his or her regular sermon. Children are encouraged to attend worship services with their parents. The children and youth programs in a family-based church are often multigenerational with parents encouraged to attend. Often family-based ministries are house churches or cell churches.

Multigenerational Ministry Philosophy

Perhaps the most common type of ministry philosophy applied to generations is found in the multigenerational church. While numerous generations attend at the same time, each generation has its own meeting places and specific ministries. Children usually do not attend the worship service with their parents. Instead, they have nursery care, Sunday school classes, or youth groups provided for them. If the adults attend a Sunday class, it is often age or lifestyle specific. Children and youth activities are usually offered during the week, while adult activities are often segmented into groups for college students, singles (young singles/older singles), single parents, couples, men, women, half-timers or prime-timers (euphemisms for seniors). While these churches have no prohibition against intergenerational activities, they exercise very little proactive planning to make them happen.

Intergenerational Ministry Philosophy

An intergenerational philosophy differs from a multigenerational philosophy by intentionally involving as many generations as possible in the life and activities of the church. For example, several generations may regularly be involved in the worship service through music, drama, sharing, and even preaching. Children's ministries may engage and involve all other ages and generations including junior high and senior high students. Mission trips and service projects are intergenerational and intergenerational mentoring is a reality. Looking from the perspective of its entire congregation, an intergenerational church incorporates the best from each age group as they follow Jesus Christ together.

In future chapters we will develop the possibilities and potential of an intergenerational church. But first we must understand the five (with a growing sixth) generations who are attending our churches. Each of these generations has differences and similarities. The differences need to be appreciated; the similarities need to be built upon.

Part 2
Understanding Today's Generations

Chapter 3
GI Generation

American soldiers storm the beaches of Normandy in the opening scene of the movie *Saving Private Ryan*. The graphic and gruesome scenes that follow are examples of major events that shaped the lives of the GI Generation. On the jacket of his book *The Greatest Generation,* Tom Brokaw writes about the GI Generation: "They came of age during the Great Depression and the Second World War and went on to build modern America—men and women whose everyday lives of duty, honor, achievement, and courage gave us the world we have today."

The GI Generation was born between 1906 and 1924, give or take a few years. The 63 million members of this generation are our churches' true *seniors*. Each day over 1000 of them pass away, taking with them stories of lives lived during remarkable times. They are survivors of the Great Depression and victors in WWII. They founded major corporations and international ministries. They developed new suburbs and were the stay-at-home moms who raised Baby Boomers. Above all, they are a resource of wisdom that needs to be heard and captured before they are no longer with us.

GI Life Events
The oldest members of the GI Generation were children when the Titanic sank and World War I was fought.

Other GIs were children during the Great Depression that started with the stock market crash on Black Thursday, October 24, 1929. The struggles for survival during the Great Depression left an indelible imprint on the minds of many GIs. They saw Prohibition come and go and, as young adults, experienced the segregation of the races. They celebrated as the Empire State Building became the world's tallest and Charles Lindbergh flew solo across the Atlantic Ocean. They mourned the loss of Amelia Earhart as she attempted to circumvent the globe. The GI Generation saw major medical advances like the discovery of penicillin and was there when America began to emerge as a world power.

Without question, the most defining moments for the GI Generation were reserved for World War II. When the rise of Adolf Hitler, his Nazi Party and the Axis threatened to dominate the world, the GI Generations of the United States, Britain and other Allied countries rose up and fought. Battlegrounds were spread to nearly every part of the world. GIs fought in the steaming jungles of Southeast Asia, on the high seas of the South Pacific, in the streets of many European cities, and in the deserts of North Africa. When the dust settled over the rubble, millions of people had died. Virtually every life in America and around the world had been disrupted and impacted by this mega war. The map of Europe was forever altered, and the Soviet Union emerged as a world power. Traumatically, the development and use of the atomic bomb jolted the world into the nuclear age. Many GIs returned home to America desiring to leave war far behind. They took advantage of the GI Bill and flooded colleges throughout the United States.

Resolutely, GIs settled down to reshape America and gave birth to the Baby Boom or Boomer Generation.

GI Popular Culture

Technological changes and advances had a significant impact on the early decades of the GI Generation. Major inventions such as the automobile and airplane revised the GIs' concept of speed, travel, and the world. The GI Generation saw and heard silent movies become "talkies." As is often the case, people do not understand the long-term ramifications or impact of some major changes. In 1928, Joseph Schenk, then president of United Artists said, "people will not want talking pictures long."[1] For the GI Generation, radio was king. Whether it was a broadcast from the Met, the Grand Ole Opry, or Yankee Stadium, families would hover over the radio to hear every note or word. President Franklin Delano Roosevelt used the radio to have "fireside chats" with the coming-of-age GI Generation. And members of this generation were among many Americans who panicked when their radios announced the beginning of *The War of the Worlds*, Orson Welles' hoax about Martians invading earth. The uproar it caused helped to underscore the power of radio.

The Golden Age of radio also brought romance, suspense, and laughter to the lives of the GIs. CBS radio's soap opera *Our Gal Sunday* began with the scintillating question, "Can a girl from a little mining town in the West find happiness as the wife of a wealthy and titled Englishman?" Other radio soap operas, called such because they were sponsored by soap manufacturers, also caught and kept the attention of young GIs. Members of the GI Generation used their imaginations as they listened to adventure and suspense shows like *One Man's Family*, *The Shadow*, *Jack Armstrong: the All-American Boy,* and *Dick Tracy*. The GI Generation laughed at the antics of Abbott and Costello, Burns and Allen, and Crosby and Hope. One of the GI's favorite radio comedies, *Amos and Andy*, underscored the racially segregated reality of the time. Two white men, Freeman Gosden and Charles Correll, used Negro dialects to portray the two black radio characters, Amos and Andy.

The music of the GI Generation was rich and varied with the jazz of Duke Ellington, the big band sound of Benny Goodman, the crooning of Bing Crosby and Frank Sinatra, the sweet sounds of Aaron Copland and the Gershwins. Whether in black and white or color, movies were popular with the GI Generation as they graduated from the cartoon matinees of their childhood to Charlie Chaplin and *The Wonderful Wizard of Oz*. They learned about love and glamour from Clark Gable and Vivien Leigh in *Gone with the Wind*; Humphrey Bogart and Lauren Bacall in *Key Largo*; Spencer Tracy and Katherine Hepburn in many movies. GIs lived through the Golden Age of Hollywood that, to this day, has not been replicated.

The GI Generation also lived through the golden age of baseball, America's national pastime. They settled into the bleachers to watch Babe Ruth, Joe DiMaggio, Lou Gehrig, Ted Williams, Stan Musial, Bob Feller, and many other Hall of Famers perform their magic. The allegiances of cities and families were often divided between the Yankees, Dodgers, Giants, Sox, and Cubs. As the GI Generation was coming of age, professional football, basketball, and hockey were also coming of age.

GI Values and Worldviews

Generally speaking, the GI Generation is made up of friendly, optimistic people. Since they were born before television, penicillin, sound movies, rockets, traffic lights, washing machines, and plastics, their values were forged during a simpler time. GIs were around long before men walked on the moon or McDonald's erected their golden arches. Consequently, their values are more basic and less materialistic and, today, are often labeled as conservative and old-fashioned. Most members of the GI Generation hold a modern worldview, placing much faith in mankind and its problem-solving ability through science and technology. Humans can solve any quandary if enough time, energy, money, and thought are given to it. GIs place great value on hard work and a strong work ethic and see themselves as a generation of doers who worked hard to build the United States into a political, economic, and social world power. In addition to building the military-industrial complex, GIs constructed the first suburbs and, in the process, redefined American life for decades to come.

Generally conservative in their worldview and politics, most GIs would agree with late President Ronald Reagan's assessment of the former Soviet Union as The Evil Empire. They have a good guy/bad guy view of the world which isn't surprising since they had to fight the bad guys to win WWII. Their war experiences taught GIs to be fiercely patriotic and they are the ones most likely to believe *my country, right or wrong, my country*. God and country, not necessarily in this order, are important to GIs, making patriotism often seem like their primary religion. Generally speaking, they are civic-minded people who have sacrificed much for their country and do not understand why everyone doesn't do the same. It is not surprising that GIs believe in buying American and are the generation most likely to be driving an American-made car.

Placing high value on community and cooperation, the GI Generation believes in social responsibility over individual rights. They have lived a life of delayed gratification and duty before pleasure and expect an orderly society where everyone respects and honors one another and people in authority. The GI Generation's high view of marriage and family produced a relatively low divorce rate and fairly compliant children, especially for older GI parents. Even when marriages were unhappy, they usually stayed together for the sake of the children. The younger GI parents saw their Boomer teenagers and young adults challenge them as The Establishment. As their values were questioned and challenged in the 1960s and 1970s, America was traumatized. This rebellion against the authoritarian GI Generation initiated social and cultural changes and forces that are still impacting America today.

GI Spirituality

The GI Generation deals pragmatically with their faith like they do everything else. Their faith is usually personal, private, and conservative and they typically are not comfortable discussing the personal application of their faith in everyday life. Many members of the GI Generation believe in and are committed to the church and denominations. They see the church as an important institution in American society and often equate it with the building on the corner. GI spirituality is often defined by church membership and involvement. Pastors and ministers are paid professionals who are employed to *do* church by preaching, marrying, burying, and making house and hospital calls.

Since the GI Generation is primarily content learning about their faith, preaching and Sunday school are important to their church experience. They are quite comfortable with predictability and generally do not respond well to changes in church activities. The preferred worship style for most GIers is traditional with its predictable liturgy, organ music, hymns and choirs. Usually the GI Generation does not transition well to contemporary worship and may be active combatants in worship wars.

The GIs may be the last generation with a consistent commitment to foreign missions and mission organizations. They generally see the rest of the world as pagans in need of conversion which may not necessarily be to Jesus Christ and Christianity but, instead, may be to democracy or capitalism. Still, sending and supporting American and Western missionaries is their primary way of reaching the world for Jesus Christ. This approach is consistent with the GI Generation's history as the founders and leaders of such post-World War II ministries as Youth for Christ, The Navigators, Campus Crusade for Christ, Young Life, and the Billy Graham Association. Institutional and organizational approaches to ministry have always been and still are important to GIs. Of all of today's generations, they hold the strongest ties to society's organizations and institutions. Subsequent generations, starting with the Silent Generation, are more fickle and selective in their organizational affiliations.

GI Generation Today

Each day, many members of the GI Generation step into eternity. While many are very active, many others have slowed down. Younger generations should glean wisdom from GIs before they leave us, gathering and recording their life experiences in writing, pictures, audio and video recordings. While they are far from perfect, GIs have experienced much, learned much, and have much to teach. This connection to the past is important for all generations.

Younger church members must be there for GI Generation in a variety of ways. For many GIs, changes in society and the world has made life seem more dangerous. Physical safety, both from violence and injury, is a major concern for many GI seniors. Regular communication and contact with younger people is important for GIs, especially if they live alone. They should be treated with respect, even when it seems that they have little to offer others.

Despite their dwindling numbers, the GI Generation is not going away quietly. Many GIs believe that they have given much to America and feel that government should take care of them in old age. Through AARP (formerly the American Association of Retired People), the Gray Panthers, and many other organizations, the GI Generation have leveraged their influence to see that their concerns and needs are addressed by society. High on their list of concerns is healthcare, especially the increasing costs of prescription drugs. Since a high percentage of the GI Generation votes, campaigning politicians still place significant value on their issues.

It is important that our churches do not push the GI Generation aside or forget about them. Since the perspectives and needs of GIs are usually different from those of the other generations, it is easy for younger church leaders to overlook them. There are numerous ways that members of the congregation can minister to GIs in the intergenerational church. We will visit this topic later.

Chapter 4
Silent Generation

The almost 50 million members of the Silent Generation have lived in the large, heroic shadow of the GI Generation. Born between 1925 and 1943, the Silent Generation is the quietest of today's living generations. For example, after seven consecutive GI Generation U.S. presidents, American voters skipped over the Silent Generation to elect Boomer presidents beginning with Bill Clinton. (The run of GI Generation Presidents started with John F. Kennedy, a WWII veteran, and ended with George H.W. Bush, also a WWII veteran.) This presidential example is representative of the Silent Generation's innocuous impact. Despite their muted leadership, Silents have contributed significantly to today's America. Let's get to know the Silent Generation better.

Silent Life Events

As children, the Silent Generation lived through the residual consequences of the Great Depression and experienced a nation at war. These two traumatic events helped to define this generation. Because of their parents' preoccupation with these two major historic events, many members of the Silent Generation were raised in an overprotected environment in which they were to be seen and not heard. These destabilizing world events also led to fewer babies and, consequently, the Silent Generation is considerably smaller than the Boomer Generation that followed.

After World War II many Silents hopped on the roaring train of a growing U.S. economy. The GI Generation returnees were *building* and *leading* corporations and a military-industrial complex, and they gave the Silent Generation the job of *managing* these new organizations. Because of a growing, healthy economy and relative social stability, members of the Silent Generation were able to stay on the job with companies for 25, 30, or even 40 years. In fact, the Silents may be the last American generation to experience such long-term job stability.

While the Korean War (1950-53) was a significant event in the lives of the Silent Generation, it did not have the status of WWII or the social impact of the Vietnam War. By comparison, the Korean War was a quieter, undeclared war that was actually called a police action. In this conflict, the Silents obediently did the bidding of and the fighting for their GI leaders. But the unsatisfying end of the Korean War resolved little and only deepened the divisions of the Cold War. Global tensions increased and the United States, the Soviet Union, and China became involved in a dangerous nuclear standoff. Consequently, the Silent Generation was the first generation to come of age under the cloud of a potential worldwide nuclear disaster. As school children and teenagers they were naively taught to duck and cover under unprotecting desks. The dark shadow of McCarthyism also taught them to duck and cover when it came to politics. To this day, the Silent Generation has yet to find its own clear voice in our society.

Despite a lack of defined leadership, the Silent Generation made major contributions to the civil rights movement. Led by Martin Luther King Jr., a Silent Generation member, they lent their momentum to a struggle that produced the 1964 Civil Rights Act. This landmark legislation prohibited racial discrimination in employment, publicly owned facilities, union membership, and federally funded programs. When President Lyndon Johnson signed the act into law he asked Americans to "eliminate the last vestiges of injustice in America." Many members of the Silent Generation resonated with these words. Generally speaking, Silents are *peacemakers* who have an innate sense of fairness and want people to get along. Consistent with the non-confrontational style of the Silent Generation, Martin Luther King would have preferred that his civil rights objectives be achieved through nonviolence.

Notably, the breakup of the Soviet Union took place with the confrontation of a GI Generation U.S. president, Ronald Reagan, and a Silent Generation Soviet leader, Mikhail Gorbachev. While too much can be made of this example, it is interesting to speculate how generational differences may have been at work here. At any rate, it is helpful and instructive to look at various historical and daily events from a generational point of view. General characteristics of various generations are at work more often than we think.

Silent Popular Culture

As mentioned previously, the parents of the Silent Generation raised their children to be seen and not heard and taught them to obey and conform at a young age.

Much of their childhood creativity was suffocated as their elders wrestled with the twin giants of the Great Depression and World War II. Despite the fact that they were the first true teenagers, they generally did not rebel. Prior to the Silent Generation, young people began working at an early age and *adolescence* did not exist. For the first time, Silents were allowed to delay adulthood as they received a high school and, sometimes, college education.

As "bobby sockers" they danced to the Big Band music of Benny Goodman and Glenn Miller. The Jitterbug and the Lindy help the Silents expend youthful energy. Members in the second half of their generation heard their favorite music by putting a nickel in a jukebox or by listening to the *Hit Parade Show* on the radio. Without television, the radio was a primary source of entertainment for the Silent Generation. They woke to the sounds of *The Breakfast Club* and laughed to the antics of Abbott and Costello and Red Skelton. The Silent Generation used their imaginations to visualize the adventures of *Superman* and *Captain Midnight*. They cowered to the stories of *The Shadow* and *The Whistler* and rode the range with Gene Autry, Roy Rogers, and the Lone Ranger. Many of their radio voices transitioned to the black-and-white screen of early television. The Silents could now see George Burns and Gracie Allen, Jack Benny, Bob Hope, Groucho Marx, and Milton Berle. Now they could both hear and see Dinah Shore, Bing Crosby, and Frank Sinatra.

As the Silent Generation was coming of age, technology began to change the way Americans lived. In addition to TV, transistor radios helped to transform the lives of Silents. Now their music became portable and personal. The coincidental emergence of television, the transistor radio, and rock and roll laid the foundation for a pop culture that would greatly impact the world for generations to come. While mostly younger Silents were affected by the birth of rock and roll, it is interesting to note that many early R&R stars were older members of their generation. They included Chuck Berry, Antoine "Fats" Domino, Jerry Lee Lewis, Roy Orbison, Bill Haley and the Comets, and, of course, Elvis Presley. The ringmaster of this new music was the venerable Silent, Dick Clark of *American Bandstand* fame.

The Silent Generation gave the "Big Screen" a variety of personalities: Marilyn Monroe, Shirley Temple, Elizabeth Taylor, Clint Eastwood, Paul Newman, Robert Redford, and Harrison Ford. On TV, many Silents became well known to their Boomer Generation audience as they starred in classic shows. For example, there was Andy Griffith in Mayberry, N.C.; Bob Keeshan as Captain Kangaroo; Florence Henderson as the mother of the Brady Bunch; and Alan Alda as *M*A*S*H*'s Dr. Hawkeye Pierce. Gen Xers were entertained and taught by Silent Generation members as they visited Fred Rogers in *Mr. Roger's Neighborhood* and laughed to the antics of Jim Henson's Muppets on *Sesame Street*.

The Silent Generation laughed at the wit of Woody Allen, the deadpan delivery of Bob Newhart, the intelligent humor of Bill Cosby, and the slapstick antics of Carol Burnett. By the standards of the generations that followed, the humor of the Silent Generation was quite *silent*. As with every generation there are some members who do not fit the mold. A number of Silents have made their mark by being more adventurous and less conforming than their peers. Hugh Hefner is a GI/Silent cusper whose Playboy empire flew in the face of the prevailing morality. Gloria Steinem and Betty Friedan worked to liberate women from their socially defined roles. James Dean was a rebel without a cause who outwardly expressed the inward frustrations, rebellion, and loneliness that his generation was unable to speak or act out. In addition, Elvis wiggled his hips within sight of many disapproving parents, and Evel Knievel displayed enough risk taking, daring, and thrill seeking for his whole generation.

The members of the Silent Generation married younger and had children earlier than any of the other generations. On average, men were 23 and women 20 years of age when they entered into matrimony. More than 90 percent of Silent women had children and stayed home to raise them. Most of their 3.3 children grew up to be late members of the Boomer Generation and early members of Generation X. Despite, or perhaps because of their controlled lifestyle, Silent couples started the divorce epidemic that has only recently leveled off.

As many Silents entered mid-life they experienced considerable angst and anxiety. Gail Sheehy explored and chronicled their unsure journey in her best-selling book *Passages*. While there are some consistent themes in adulthood, such as relationships, sexuality, aging, and spirituality, subsequent generations have not necessarily gone through the adult lifecycle in the same ways as the Silents. Another popular book from the 1970s that described the world of Silents was Daniel Levinson's *The Seasons of a Man's Life*. Like *Passages* this book describes stages in the lives of Silent Generation men. While both of these books targeted Silents, they have been very helpful in initiating the study and understanding of the adult years for other generations.

Business for the Silent Generation was a man's world. Actually, it was "the organization man's" world. William Whyte's 1956 book called *The Organization Man* described the experience of white males in the Silent Generation. The book defines organization men as "the ones of our middle class who have left home, spiritually as well as physically, to take the vows of organization life, and it is they who are the mind and soul of our great self-perpetuating institutions." [1] Many Silent Generation men spent their working years as organization men in America's growing corporations. True to their *play it safe* philosophy, less than 5 percent of Silents ventured out to become self-employed.

As mentioned previously, the most striking political failing of the Silents is that no U.S. President has yet come from this generation, but not because they haven't tried. The list of unsuccessful presidential hopefuls from the Silent Generation is long: Robert F. Kennedy, Walter Mondale, Michael Dukakis, Ross Perot, Pat Robertson, Ted Kennedy, Pat Buchanan, Jesse Jackson, Jerry Brown, Gary Hart, Ralph Nader, John McCain, and more. Since America elected GI Generation presidents from John F. Kennedy to George Bush (Sr.) and then elected Boomers presidents, Bill Clinton, George W. Bush and generational cusper Barack Obama, it is quite possible that America will never have a Silent Generation president.

Nevertheless, the Silent Generation is not without heroes. As the United States raced the Soviet Union to the moon, a group of Silents stepped forward to become America's first astronauts. It was Silent Generation member

Neil Armstrong who became the first human to set foot on the moon's surface. After his historic feat, Armstrong faded into the background in good Silent Generation fashion and only in his later years did he agree to have his biography written. The names of other Silent Generation astronauts became familiar to many Americans, including Scott Carpenter, Gus Grissom, Gordon Cooper, Frank Borman, and Buzz Aldrin.

Silent Values and Worldviews

Most Silent Generation members grew up in difficult times. As mentioned, the older Silents experienced the brunt of both the Great Depression and World War II, while the younger Silents were more influenced by WWII as children and adolescents. Because of these tough times, family survival became a priority for the parents of Silent Generation children. Many parents made it clear to their children that they were making sacrifices so the Silents could grow up in a world of peace and prosperity. And the Silent Generation *did* come of age during a time of growing peace and prosperity. Consequently, some members of the Silent Generation feel guilty because life wasn't as difficult as it was for their parents. As a result, many Silents believe they have an obligation to make the world a better place.

Their turbulent early years have also shaped the values and attitudes of the Silent Generation in other ways. Perhaps the major characteristic of this generation is their adaptability. The average Silent generally does not force his or her feelings and desires upon a situation. Instead, Silents generally adapt to changing situations. Also, because many grew up as suffocated and overprotected children, the Silents are a low risk-taking generation, generally opting to play it safe. Because they have worked hard and behaved themselves, Silents expect to be rewarded for their loyalty, conformity, and diligence. Since most chose to work for companies, corporations, educational, or governmental institutions, many have retired comfortably with good pensions and investments.

Another value of the Silent Generation is their desire to keep the peace, often at any cost. Most Silents do not work well within an environment of conflict and confrontation. Rather, they believe that problems should be addressed peacefully and orderly and should be resolved in ways that make everyone happy. As a result, they believe it is important to make decisions based on consensus. Silents often do not understand the passionate agendas held by members of other generations and can have difficulty in decision-making meetings involving Boomers and Gen Xers. Since members of the Silent Generation have a broader sense of community and want to be inclusive, they are not strong-minded decision makers. Instead, they can make good mediators.

As parents, many Silent Generation members were also passive and non-confrontational. They often thought that if they just worked hard and provided a good home for their children, everything would work out all right. Unfortunately for Silents, their Boomer and Gen X children needed more than custodial parenting. Today, many members of the Silent Generation find themselves out of sync with younger generations and with social and global changes. Their adaptive qualities do not serve them as well today as in the past. Consequently, many Silents have simplified their lives by narrowing their involvements. They have chosen their friends, identified their desired activities, and shut out background noise. You generally will not find Silents leading social change today. Instead, they choose to work on specific projects and ventures where they will be most helpful and see concrete results.

Silent Spirituality

Because of their values of fairness, tolerance, and compassion, the Silents are often the nice people in a church who want to include everyone in church activities. But their pluralistic bent is a two-edged sword. While concerned about most everyone, Silents are not decisive and visionary when it comes to ministry decisions and direction. Unlike crusading Boomers, most Silents are content to have a spiritual impact on their grandchildren rather than to change the world.

While many Silents enjoy contemporary worship, most prefer a traditional style. Along with the remaining GIs, they are major combatants in the worship wars. Many Silents believe that true worship happens with an organ, hymns, and a robed choir. In local churches where Silents represent the majority of church leaders who insist on traditional worship, fewer younger generation attendees are found. And without the infusion of younger congregants, many churches will slowly die as they insist on business as usual.

The Silent Generation also approaches their spiritual lives or "spiritual formation" in unique ways. Bible study experiences, whether in large or small groups, are important to Silents. As churchgoers, they place great importance on lifelong learning. More than the generations that follow, Silents still enjoy being taught by authoritative teachers in a traditional Sunday school format. In fact, they may be the last generation that sits quietly and listens to a teacher. Younger generations, on the other hand, need action, interaction, and discussion or they will generally not attend such classes.

Silent Generation members are often quite reserved about sharing the details of their spiritual lives. Like GIers, they see spirituality as personal and private. Nonetheless, Silents are generally committed to the church as a significant community institution and, today, form the backbone of many congregations. As the wealthiest generation ever, they are major financial contributors to the work of church and parachurch ministries. In light of their generally quiet and private spirituality, it is interesting to speculate how and why so many Silent Generation members have been controversial Christians. A partial answer is found in the wedding of ministry with television and other media outlets. The possibilities of reaching millions of people with their message have produced high-profile Silents such as Pat Robertson, Jerry Falwell, Jim and Tammy Faye Bakker, James Dobson, Jimmy Swaggert, and Benny Hinn. The ministry efforts of these Silents have given Christianity a unique and dubious American flavor.

Silent Generation Today

In the new millennium, the Silent Generation has emerged as a new breed of American elders. They are our first generation of *young old*. Most Silents are retired and they may spend several decades in retirement. But unlike their generational predecessors, the thought of entitlement will not rest easy on the minds of many well-heeled Silents. Instead, their propensity to help others may usher in a new age of private philanthropy. It also may yield a large number of volunteers who want to be actively involved in ministry and nonprofit activities. The Silent Generation is made up of doers who need something specific and defined to do, so they can see the concrete results of their labor.

As a whole, the Silents are the wealthiest generation in American history. They gently rode the wave of postwar prosperity to financial freedom. The Silent Generation knows about profit sharing, pensions, job security, annual raises, and retirement plans. But their perception and understanding of the needs of others, including their children and grandchildren, may keep many Silents from enjoying their retirement years. Since many Silents are first-class worriers about the future, constantly changing economic realities cause many Silents to worry about outliving their retirement resources. Other Silents have no problem putting a "Spending Our Children's Inheritance" bumper sticker on the back of their expensive RV.

Many members of the Silent Generation are active grandparents. In fact, about four million grandparents are currently raising their grandchildren. In addition, many Silents are increasingly joining multigenerational households that include their children and grandchildren. Even if they do not live in a multigenerational household, they are often the glue that holds their extended family together. Many Silents, especially men, have seized a second opportunity to do parenting better with their grandchildren.

Now in their sixties, seventies, and eighties Silents want to experience those things they had deferred. Many remain in good health and will use their free time to enjoy life and do good. Since they represent a wealth of experience and knowledge, Silents can be major contributors to the ministry of a local church. They are capable of handling significant and concrete ministry tasks and should be given more than menial, time-filling duties. Churches that take the time to understand and appreciate the Silent Generation will gain a valuable ministry partner.

Chapter 5
Boomer Generation

The Boomer Generation started it all: No one paid much attention to generations until Baby Boomers came along. When the 78 million Boomers exploded on the American scene, all of society took notice. This generation's many monikers served notice that they were something special. Also known as the Baby Boom Generation, the Spock Generation, TV Generation, Hippies, Yuppies, Flower Children, and the Vietnam Generation, the Boomer Generation has always seen itself as special. Even today, Boomers continue to draw attention to themselves. Because of their size, influence, and buying power, demographers and marketers continue to treat the Boomer Generation as America's 800-pound gorilla. In short, much of the interest in today's generations started with a study of the Boomers.

The first members of the Boomer Generation were born in 1944, the last in 1962. (As with all generations, some cuspers may exhibit the characteristics of the generation that precedes or follows them.) With the end of World War II, returning veterans set out to establish families and build a life of peace and prosperity. Consequently, America experienced the largest birth rate in the nation's history. But as we will see, the Boomers did not give America or their parents much peace.

Peter Menconi

Boomer Life Events

Most Boomers grew up during the optimistic post-war years of the 1950s and early 1960s as America was on a roll. The economy was growing; there was little unemployment; America was becoming a superpower; family life was generally happy and simple. Even with the ever-present Cold War, most Americans moved on to build a good life for themselves and their families. After all, the Cold War was better than a shooting war. Little did the adults know that the young Boomers would soon question this tranquil and bland lifestyle.

President John F. Kennedy's idealism fueled the expectations of this new generation. At his inaugural address on January 20, 1961 he challenged the nation to "ask not what your country can do for you—ask what you can do for your country." With its idealism, glamour, and mystique, his short administration came to be known as *Camelot*, after the Broadway musical popular at that time. (After his death, Jackie Kennedy revealed that her husband's favorite line from the musical was "Don't let it be forgot, that once there was a spot, for one brief shining moment, that was known as Camelot.") The Kennedys' Camelot was dawning as the oldest Boomers entered college. But this new vision of America would not be given much time to develop, for President Kennedy would soon be dead. (Most Boomers can tell you where they were and what they were doing when they heard the news of President Kennedy's assassination.) In many ways, the assassination of JFK on November 22, 1963 was the event that triggered the Boomer Generation. This traumatic event, along with the ongoing civil rights movement and the growing Vietnam War, created rumblings of social change within America.

In August 1963, Martin Luther King Jr. boomed out his famous "I have a dream" speech from the steps of the Lincoln Memorial and across the Mall packed with motivated protestors. At that rally a young folksinger named Bob Dylan sang about "the day Medgar Evers was buried from a bullet that he caught." Joan Baez sang the civil rights anthem *We Shall Overcome*. And Jackie Robinson promised, "we cannot be turned back." Within this atmosphere of social change the first half of the Boomer Generation was coming of age—"the times they are a-changin'."

The 1960s became one of the most colorful periods in American history. Long hair, tie-dyed shirts, bell-bottomed jeans and other manners of bizarre dress (and undress) were commonplace. "Make love, not war" became the anthem of the flower children who flooded San Francisco during the Summer of Love in 1967. The following song was a siren call that lured many young Boomers from America's East Coast and heartland to the West Coast:

San Francisco
(Be Sure To Wear Some Flowers In Your Hair)
Written by John Phillips.
Performed by Scott McKenzie.
Published by MCA Music Publishing, a Division of MCA, Inc.
Courtesy of Epic Records.
Released June 10, 1967.

If you're going to San Francisco
Be sure to wear some flowers in your hair

Peter Menconi

If you're going to San Francisco
You're gonna meet some gentle people there
For those who come to San Francisco
Summertime will be a love-in there
In the streets of San Francisco
Gentle people with flowers in their hair
All across the nation,
such a strange vibration
People in motion
There's a whole generation,
with a new explanation
People in motion, people in motion
For those who come to San Francisco
Be sure to wear some flowers in your hair
If you come to San Francisco
Summertime will be a love-in there
If you come to San Francisco
Summertime will be a love-in there

Whether they considered themselves flower children or not, most young Boomers were aware and concerned about a number of important issues. They wrestled with such controversial topics as civil rights, the environment, personal and sexual freedom, nuclear arms, and the Vietnam War. Years later, Abbie Hoffman, co-founder of the Youth International Party (YIP a.k.a. Yippies), activist, anarchist and one of the notorious Chicago Seven, wrote about these times:

We are here to make a better world.

No amount of rationalization or blaming can preempt the moment of choice each of us brings to our situation here

60

on this planet. The lesson of the 60's is that people who cared enough to do right could change history.

We didn't end racism but we ended legal segregation.

We ended the idea that you could send half-a-million soldiers around the world to fight a war that people do not support.

We ended the idea that women are second-class citizens.

We made the environment an issue that couldn't be avoided.

The big battles that we won cannot be reversed. We were young, self-righteous, reckless, hypocritical, brave, silly, head-strong, and scared half to death.

And we were right.

Though their passion may be diluted, many older Boomers still hold Hoffman's image of their generation… they still think they can change the world.

In the mid-1960s, the Vietnam War demanded more and more American involvement. As thousands of American soldiers returned home in body bags, colleges and universities across the United States began to stir. In New York, Chicago, Madison, Boulder, Berkeley, and elsewhere, students seized control of administration buildings in protest to the war. Other antiwar protestors stormed the Pentagon and other federal buildings in frustration over the escalating conflict and increasing deaths. Politicians became greatly divided over the war and whether to continue it.

Then came 1968, a year that left an indelible imprint on the minds of older Boomers. The year started with the Tet Offensive in which the Viet Cong launched successful surprise attacks against American and South Vietnamese troops. Americans began to realize that we could actually lose this war. Leading up to the November election the presidential candidates were hotly debating policy on the war. Then on April 4, 1968, Martin Luther King Jr. was assassinated and black anger erupted in the streets of Chicago, Baltimore, Cincinnati and Washington D.C.. Despite 5,000 troops dispatched to keep order in the Chicago streets, many people died or were injured in the rioting. Meanwhile, other American cities burned. Two months later, on June 5, 1968, presidential candidate Senator Robert F. Kennedy was assassinated.

America was to experience even more trauma in 1968. During August's Democratic National Convention in Chicago, antiwar demonstrators converged on the city and the chaos within the convention hall was outdone only by the bedlam in the streets outside the hall. Hundreds of policemen armed with nightsticks and tear gas charged protestors marching to the convention hall. More than one hundred people, including children, elderly, and members of the press, were injured. On their TV screens, Americans now saw Americans fighting themselves; it seemed like the country was coming unraveled.

As the 1960s were drawing to a close, Americans watched their televisions in amazement on July 20, 1969 as Neil Armstrong became the first human to walk on the moon. As he stepped from his landing craft, he spoke the famous words, "that's one small step for man, one giant leap for mankind." Beat up from a tumultuous decade Americans needed some good news and fun. Many found it a couple of months later when a mostly Boomer crowd of nearly 400,000 swarmed through the small town of Bethel,

N.Y. to a music festival on a 600-acre dairy farm. The Woodstock festival became an enduring symbol of the Boomer Generation. Festival goers heard music from such rock icons as Richie Havens; Jefferson Airplane; Grateful Dead; Crosby, Stills, Nash and Young; Creedence Clearwater Revival; The Who; The Band; Janis Joplin; and Jimi Hendrix.

The 1960s began as an idealistic decade with President Kennedy challenging Americans to commit themselves to national and international service. The new frontier he envisioned was to take many turbulent twists by the end of the decade. As the 1960s drew to a close, the United States was a very different nation. America had weathered the assassinations of its leaders, riots and protests in its streets, an unpopular war in a far-off Asian nation, and the emergence of the Boomer Generation. Now young Americans were sporting long hair and mod clothes while espousing antiestablishment ideas. Drug use and sexual freedom were commonplace and a counterculture had emerged that looked nothing like the vision of Camelot.

As the 1970s began, the Boomer Generation was shocked by the killings at Kent State University and the breakup of the Beatles. At about the same time, the unruly behavior of the Chicago Seven in the courtroom exemplified the irreverent and confrontational attitudes of many young Boomers. The Boomer Generation challenged the norms and mores of the GI and Silent Generations. The impact and implication of this countercultural change took root and defined the 1970s decade. By 1971, one-third of American students had tried marijuana and one-in-seven were regular smokers. The rise in drug use, especially heroin, was punctuated by the overdose deaths of Jimi Hendrix and Janis Joplin. Meanwhile, the related sexual revolution changed many lives. Laws forbidding abortions were over-turned, and birth control pills and methods led to more promiscuous behavior. More homosexuals "came out of the closet," and the divorce rate among couples moved rapidly upward.

In the first half of the 1970s the antiwar movement and pressure from the North Vietnamese army and the Viet Cong caused America to take another look at the war. After numerous failed attempts at peace negotiations, American forces pulled out of Vietnam and Saigon fell to the Communists on April 30, 1975. Returning GIs were not welcomed home as heroes as they were after World War II. Even today many Boomer Generation Vietnam veterans are tormented by the aftereffects of an unpopular and, to many, shameful war. The Vietnam War was a defining life event for many Boomers. The possibility of being drafted into military service sent many males of the Boomer Generation to college and forced others to Canada. When many Boomers today look back and recall the days of the Vietnam War, their stomachs churn.

In 1973 Watergate and the Arab oil embargo further reinforced the cynicism among many in the Boomer Generation. These events only underscored for Boomers that the establishment was corrupt and greedy. President Richard Nixon's disgraceful resignation was followed by his controversial pardon by President Gerald Ford. To compound matters, inflation was rampant and the nation's economy had stalled. The malaise of the 1970s was briefly interrupted by the glorious celebration of America's 200th birthday. But

Jimmy Carter's presidency in the late 1970s only seemed to deepen the gloominess of the time.

By the time the 1980s arrived Boomers were ready for change, but not necessarily the change that followed. Promising to put America back to work again, Ronald Reagan was elected the 40th president of the nation on November 4, 1980. Many Americans were ready to go *back to the future* and return to the values of the 1950s. A month after the election, the shooting death of John Lennon made real a line from one of his songs: "The dream is over." President Reagan himself was wounded in an assassination attempt about four months after Lennon's death. The following year, Pope John Paul II was shot and wounded in St. Peter's Square. Crazed individuals, taking history into their own hands, foreshadowed the future terrorism that was to come.

The early 1980s also saw the emergence of the religious right movement. Starting with the Moral Majority, many organizations began to wed fundamentalist and evangelical religious views with political clout. Issues such as teen pregnancy, abortion, crime, homosexuality, political corruption, and drugs mobilized the religious right. Over time, the religious right began to include politically conservative Catholics, Jews, Mormons, and others. Together they opposed such issues as the Equal Rights Amendment, abortion and gay rights. In addition, the religious right supported prayer in the schools, traditional Christian and family values, and abstinence among the unmarried. The Christian right was led by such energetic Silent Generation figures as Jerry Falwell, Pat Robertson, Phyllis Schlafly, William Bennett, and James Dobson.

The culture wars had begun. While many Boomers supported the culture wars that developed, many did not. The cultural debate that raged during the 1980s polarized the nation. Thoughtful Christians, and Americans in general, were often forced to choose sides. The religious right advocated a return to traditional values. Traditional values were usually defined as the importance of family life, hard work, respect for authority, patriotism, and good citizenship. To opponents, a return to traditional values sounded like a return to 1950s values and they were having none of it. Instead, the cultural left was proposing the adoption of political correctness where diverse lifestyles and values were embraced with equal enthusiasm. The culture wars have raged for nearly 30 years and have hastened the erosion of the religious and political middle.

As the 1980s drew to a close, there was a surge of democracy around the world. Boomers and other generations watched helplessly as pro-democracy demonstrators were massacred in Beijing's Tiananmen Square. The Soviet empire began to crumble as one bloc nation after another cast off the shackles of Communism. Then in November 1989, the Berlin Wall, the Cold War's most enduring symbol, was reduced to rubble. Most Boomers had spent their whole lives under the threat of the nuclear war with the Soviets—and now it was over.

The 1990s began with a new sense of optimism and enthusiasm. The evil empire was gone and the United States stood alone as the world's only true superpower. But America's military might was soon tested as Saddam Hussein's forces invaded Kuwait. Boomers and their families watched in amazement, as Operation Desert Storm became the first made-for-TV war. Smart bombs introduced the world to new technological warfare. After 100 hours of ground operations, American and coalition forces freed Kuwait.

Technology would play a big part in Boomers and all Americans lives in the 1990s. Computers began to profoundly change the way Americans worked and played. The widespread use of the Internet and e-mail changed the way Boomers and others shopped, conducted business, received information, and communicated. Cell phones and the availability of inexpensive worldwide communication began to make the world a smaller place. The world was truly becoming a global village. Most Boomers adapted well to technological changes. In fact, many Boomers such as Microsoft's Bill Gates and Apple's Steve Jobs helped lead the digital revolution. In the second half of the 1990s, technology companies and their stocks became the rage among many investors. As the stock indices soared, even conservative investors wanted a piece of the action. When the stock market bubble burst in 2000, many Boomers hopes of an early retirement burst with it.

Starting in 1993, the presidency of a Boomer, Bill Clinton, would have a profound impact on the moral and ethical psyche of Americans. His sexual exploits while in office left a scar on his presidency and fueled debate on morality among average Americans. As an early Boomer, Clinton's behavior reflected a generation that had produced a sexual revolution that has profoundly changed America. The practical impact of the sexual revolution was the high rate of divorce that swept across America, and Generation X was to bear the brunt of this seismic change.

Peter Menconi

Another life event that affected the Boomer Generation was the ending of one millennium and the start of another. As the new millennium approached, many Boomers and other Americans feared major breakdowns in society caused by our computers' inability to navigate the date change from 12/31/99 to 1/1/00. Many people stockpiled water, food, and fuel to ensure survival if society returned to the days of pre-1900 America. The fears proved unwarranted and the world celebrated the arrival of a new millennium with much pomp, circumstance, and brilliant fireworks.

The new millennium was to bring a new world. A new Boomer president, George W. Bush, was at the helm of the United States when terrorists attacked Americans on American soil. The events of September 11, 2001 shattered any remaining naiveté that the world was a safe place. The Boomer Generation, along with the other living generations, were now faced with the task of navigating life through a new mine field planted by terrorists. The 9/11 attacks led to subsequent military actions in Afghanistan and Iraq. In response to these events, many Boomers and other Americans rethought the priorities of their lives. Many Americans' initial response to 9/11 was to spend more time at home and cocoon. Today, it appears that many of these changes have eroded.

Boomer Popular Culture

The Boomer Generation has experienced a rich variety of cultural changes, many of which are owed to technology, especially television. Virtually all members of the Boomer Generation do not remember a world without TV.

Its pervasiveness in the lives of Boomers has profoundly affected their view of the world, and much of what they learned as children has come through their TV sets. The universe of young Boomers was expanded and shaped by Howdy Doody, Captain Kangaroo, and the Mouseketeers. Their imaginations were fueled by the original *Wonderful World of Disney*. Many learned how adults and parents—other than theirs—acted by watching *I Love Lucy, The Honeymooners, Father Knows Best,* and *Leave it to Beaver.* Many young Boomers laughed at the antics of Lucy and Ricky Ricardo as they lived through the trials and tribulations of marriage. They were also entertained by the exploits of Jackie Gleason as Ralph Kramden and his famous bellow, "One of these days, one of these days…POW! RIGHT IN THE KISSER!"

The televised Nixon-Kennedy debates in 1960 ushered in a whole new era of politics and political campaigning. Now, TV became a major tool for politicians and campaigning. On November 22, 1963, all regular TV programming was suspended as the networks brought the nation coverage of John Kennedy's assassination. Television brought the nation together through this crisis. Boomers grew to expect that world events would come into their homes through this amazing technology. Certainly, the Vietnam War became the first war shown on TV. (Later, in the second war in Iraq, TV reporters would be embedded with troops and give us real time views of combat.) The rapid availability of information on the war allowed for immediate political responses on all sides of the issue and television allowed the whole world to watch the conflict unfold.

Peter Menconi

Much more of the Boomers' pop culture was shaped by television. In the mid-1950s, *American Bandstand* hit the national airwaves. A predecessor to MTV, *American Bandstand* helped set the standard for what was cool among teenagers. Each weekday afternoon millions of adolescents would tune in to see the "regulars" on *American Bandstand* introduce the latest dance steps: The Stroll, The Twist, The Slop, The Hand Jive, and The Bop. Teenagers across the country knew the names of all the *AB* regulars—who was dating who and when they broke up. It became important to look and dance like the teens on *American Bandstand*. Dick Clark, the show's ageless host, would introduce teenagers to the latest and hottest artists. Reruns of *AB* may look quaint today, but the program set in motion the profound influence the media was to have on subsequent generations of adolescents.

Boomer pop culture was further fueled by the appearances of Elvis Presley and the Beatles on *The Ed Sullivan Show*. This "really big shooow" was the premiere variety series that placed millions of Boomers and their families in front of their TVs each Sunday night from 1948 to 1971. The popularity of the Beatles in America was given a boost by their appearance on the show. On February 9, 1964, with over 70 million people watching, the Fab Four sang *I Want to Hold Your Hand* and *She Loves You*. Other English bands such as the Rolling Stones contributed to the British invasion of pop music in the second half of the 1960s. Once again, television was a powerful force in driving popular culture.

The Boomer Generation experienced a wide variety of musical genre as they were coming of age. In the 1950s and early 1960s, classic rock and roll—led by Elvis Presley— was the Boomers' music of choice. Along with rock and roll came the "greaser culture," later portrayed in the TV show *Happy Days* with The Fonz as the stereotypic greaser. This subculture was celebrated by Hollywood in *American Graffiti* and *Grease*. For some older Boomers, folk music became popular and laid the pop-cultural foundation for coming social change. Artist such as Peter, Paul and Mary, Joan Baez, Judy Collins, and the Kingston Trio popularized music that had a social conscience. Then Bob Dylan took folk music to a new level. Not only was his music widely popular, but it often carried a message of social change that resonated with Boomers.

Another music stream was to emerge in the 1960s that introduced black music to white audiences. The Motown sound that came out of Detroit conquered America and the world. Motown music gave African-American Boomers a voice that developed along with the civil rights movement. This unique music launched such stars as The Tempations, Diana Ross and The Supremes, Stevie Wonder, Smokey Robinson, and Marvin Gaye. The Motown sound influenced many music artists, both black and white, who followed. The 1970s gave us Michael Jackson and the Jackson 5, as well as the racially mixed band of Sly and the Family Stone who created a pop-soul-rock hybrid that had Boomers dancing. In the 1970s an inner city black sound called "funk" hit the music scene. The late James Brown and Kool and the Gang popularized this sound for both black and white audiences.

The Beatles split up at the beginning of the 1970s and several new types of music took hold. A blending of folk and rock music, popularized by such artists as Simon and Garfunkel, formed a bridge from the 1960s to the 1970s. The Osmonds and the Carpenters produced a sentimental sound called "soft rock" that had its own following of Boomers. A number of mainstream troubadours including James Taylor, Carly Simon, and Jackson Browne gave Boomers songs with intensely personal lyrics. Pop rock groups such as Fleetwood Mac, the Doobie Brothers, the Eagles, and Chicago produced a middle-of-the-road style that many called "corporate rock." Also during this time, Elton John provided his own version of entertaining music together with outrageous costumes and behavior. Taking outrageousness to a new level, Kiss and other bands introduced "shock rock" with its over-the-top theatrics. Other punk and heavy metal rock groups such as Black Sabbath and Led Zepplin introduced destructive undercurrents into pop music that influenced a segment of the Boomer Generation, especially the second-half Boomers.

By the mid-1970s, most of the 1960s idealism was gone and the impact of profound social upheaval was settling in. The 1970s was a cynical time for many Boomers. Those who were coming of age during this time saw the firsthand impact of drug abuse, a spiraling divorce rate, and a bleak economy. Disco music appeared in the 1970s and helped provide some levity to this dismal period. Boomers danced to the sounds of the Bee Gees, the Village People, and Donna Summers, the undisputed diva of disco. The disco lifestyle was unforgettably strobe-lit in the movie *Saturday Night Fever* with white-suited John Travolta playing the part of aspiring dancer Tony Mancro.

In addition to TV and music, the movies had a profound effect on the views of Boomers. As America moved from the gentler 1950s to the chaotic and turbulent 1960s, movies carried messages and had an "edge." Movies such as *Psycho, The Manchurian Candidate, Dr. Strangelove, Bonnie and Clyde, Easy Rider, Midnight Cowboy, The Graduate, and 2001: A Space Odyssey* changed the way movies were made. The movies of the 1960s also stretched the standard of what was acceptable on the big screen and helped to shape the changing views of a generation. Previously accepted mores were being questioned and many movie themes from this time were about challenging authority. Consequently, Boomers were raised on different moral and ethical standards than preceding generations. The change in America's moral climate set in motion in the 1960s continues to reverberate and is even more amplified today.

Popular culture's changing morality inspired much of the social transformation that was to follow. The sexual revolution and the feminist movement contributed to the destabilization of family life and the significant increase in the divorce rate. The lives of many Boomers and Gen Xers who grew up in the 1970s and 1980s were greatly impacted by the trauma brought on by their parent's divorce, and we are still wrestling with the repercussions of these changes today.

Generation Jones

Many Boomers from the second half of the generation do not identify with the heady spiritual awakening of the 1960s. They often see themselves as different and distinct from older members of their generation. Some observers have labeled younger Boomers and cuspers born between 1956 and 1965 as *Generation Jones*. (The name, in part, is derived from a 1972 hit song, *Love Jones*.) As children this group was promised "a brave new world," but as teenagers, lived in an unstable, floundering society. Consequently, many members of Generation Jones have wed the idealistic drive of early Boomers with the self-reliance, skepticism, and noncommittal attitudes of Generation X.

The popular culture of Generation Jonesers was somewhat different than that of the first-half Boomers. Many Jonesers remember lava lamps, macramé, pet rocks, platform shoes, and blue eye-shadow with fondness—or not. They relate to the music, TV shows, and movies of the 1970s and not the 1960s. The eclectic nature of pop culture during the 1970s caused a greater splintering and segmenting of this cohort group than in previous generations. The ready availability of drugs, high crime rates, and the increasing divorce rate had profound effects on how Generation Jonesers experienced adolescence. Many Jonesers today do not clearly understand how their coming-of-age experiences have shaped the people they are today.

The life events that affected Generation Jonesers are also somewhat different than those that affected early boomers. Many later-half Boomers do not remember where they were or what they were doing when President Kennedy was assassinated and many were children during the civil rights movement and unrest. Most Jonesers were also too young to understand the turmoil created by the Vietnam War. Instead, they were more affected by the Watergate scandal, the Arab oil crisis and long gas station lines, environmental disasters, the Jonestown mass suicide, and the Iranian hostage crisis. They remember names like Ted Bundy, Patty Hearst, Jim Jones, Miss Piggy, Ayatollah Khomeini, Three Mile Island, Farrah Fawcett, Mark Spitz, Archie Bunker, Kojak, Dr. J, Bruce Jenner, and Rocky Balboa. Generation Jonesers came of age with TV shows such as *Roots, The Muppet Show, M*A*S*H, Charlie's Angels, All in the Family, Wonder Woman, Saturday Night Live,* and *The Mary Tyler Moore Show.* Some of the memorable movies for Generation Jonesers are *The Godfather, Love Story, American Graffiti, Star Wars, Alien, Dirty Harry, Patton, The Exorcist, Clockwork Orange, Apocalypse Now, Grease, Animal House,* and *Rocky.*

Some social commentators have argued that the 1970s were a time of transition between the spiritual awakening of the 1960s and the go-go years of the 1980s. More recently, other writers have described the 1970s as *the* pivotal decade that has given us the world in which we now live. In his book, *How We Got Here: The 70s—The Decade that Brought You Modern Life (For Better or Worse),* David Frum summarizes the turmoil of the decade:

> "They were strange feverish years, the 1970s. They were a time of unease and despair, punctuated by disaster. The murder of athletes at the 1972 Olympic games. Desert emirates cutting off America's oil. Military humiliation in Indochina. Criminals taking control of America's streets. The dollar plunging in value. Marriages collapsing. Drugs for sale in every high school. A president toppled from office. The worst economic slump since the Great Depression, followed four years later by the second-worst economic slump since the Depression. The U.S. government baffled as its diplomats are taken hostage. And

in the background loomed still wilder and stranger alarms and panics. The ice age was returning. Killer bees were swarming up across the Rio Grande. The world was running out of natural resources. Kahoutek's comet was hurtling toward the planet. Epidemic swine flu would carry off millions of elderly people. Karen Silkwood had been murdered for trying to warn us that nuclear reactors were poisoning the earth. General Motors was suppressing the patent on a hyper-efficient engine. Food shortages would soon force Americans to subsist on algae."[2]

The second-half Boomers, Generation Jones, came of age during this time. These life events have had a profound impact on how they see the world and why they act the way they do today.

Bruce Schulman, in his book *The Seventies: The Great Shift in American Culture, Society, and Politics*, further argues that the 1970s were responsible for two major shifts in the thinking of Americans. First, the growing middle class began to believe that entrepreneurship was the primary way to personal freedom. "During the 1970s and early 1980s, Americans concluded that capitalist accumulation was not the enemy of doing good but the vehicle for it,"[3] he writes. Secondly, Schulman argues that America in the 1970s became "southernized," meaning that low taxes, reduced social services, and military preparedness became the central themes of public policy—specifically President Reagan's public policy. It is important to understand these major shifts if one wants to understand and minister to members of Generation Jones.

Boomer Values and Worldviews

From an early age it became apparent that the Boomer Generation was not going to automatically adopt the worldview and values of either the GI Generation or the Silent Generation. Growing up during the Cold War and with the threat of nuclear warfare, most Boomers learned early that the world is not a safe place. Consequently, many Boomers were determined to change the world. The activism that resulted—a trademark of the Boomer Generation—was directed at bringing about a spiritual awakening in America. Spirituality has been, and continues to be, important to Boomers, but their spirituality is not often the type defined by the traditional Judeo-Christian values of preceding generations. Instead, many Boomers have drawn their views of spirituality from diverse religious traditions. Their spirituality is often a mixture of Hindu meditation, a sprinkle of the teachings of Jesus Christ and the Buddha, a morsel of Native American religious practices, and anything else you want to add. This eclectic view of spirituality and religion has created a challenge for churches over the past several decades. The absolute truth of orthodox Christianity has been replaced by the belief that there are many roads to God. We will take a closer look at Boomer spirituality shortly.

The changing worldviews of Boomers represented the beginning of a major transition from a modern way of looking at the world to a postmodern view. A significant number of Boomers were among the first to question modern life. The counterculture movement within the Boomer Generation was primarily an attempt, though somewhat naïve, to bring love and peace to a world that seemed crazy. The collective challenge of the Boomer Generation to their elders and the establishment has followed Boomers into midlife and beyond. Most Boomers still do not easily conform, and they continue to express their individuality in various ways. Consequently, marketers and entrepreneurs have seized on customizing products and services for Boomers. While seeming paradoxical, Boomers also believe that collectively, they can still change the world. The generation that followed the Boomer Generation does not share a similar sense of group identity. Generation X is more individualized in their values and approach to life.

Other experiences have shaped the values and worldviews of Boomers. Because they were the largest generation born in America, Boomers found themselves competing for everything: for room in daycare; space in crowded classrooms; acceptance into college; jobs upon graduating college; promotions in the workplace. They competed and continue competing in athletics, making money, staying young, and they will eventually compete for space in senior care centers. Competition is a value the Boomers will take to their graves—perhaps competing for cemetery space.

The Boomer Generation has always felt that they invented the youth culture and pop culture. So, it is not surprising that as Boomers reach middle age and beyond, they attempt to stave off aging. The Boomer Generation will not age gracefully. In fact, many Boomers see themselves as younger than their chronological age, forever young. Consequently, they have fueled the boom in cosmetic surgery, botox injections, hair replacement therapies, vitamins, food supplements, teeth whiteners, and exercise equipment. It was the Boomer Generation that popularized health and fat-free foods, diets, alternative medicines, and yoga.

Boomers also raised stress management and the search for self-actualization to new heights. They want to stay fashionable and will continue to drive a large segment of the apparel market for years to come. In an attempt to market its products and services to Boomers, the American Association of Retired Persons changed its name to AARP. Boomers will not *retire*, even when they stop working. Approaches that worked with the GI and Silent Generations did not work well with the Boomer Generation, thus, AARP has changed its strategies when marketing to Boomers. Now it offers strategies and products that assume that Boomers will stay active in the workplace and in society, focusing much less on retirement.

As the most educated generation in America's history, Boomers continue to value schooling. Many Boomers continue to seek formal and informal educational experiences even after college or graduate school. They were the first generation to recognize that lifelong learning was necessary if they wanted to stay employed. Also, Boomers sought a variety of educational experiences allowing them to change careers and do something more meaningful. Many Boomers have voiced the theme that it is very important to spend your time and energy at a career or serious avocation that makes the world a better place. As many members of the Boomer Generation enter midlife and beyond, it will not be unusual to see significant numbers return to school or get involved in world changing activities they consider important.

Marriage and family are also highly valued by Boomers. It is ironic that as adolescents and young adults, Boomers ushered in a sexual revolution that destabilized the family structure of previous generations by increasing divorce and remarriage rates and greatly altering American society. And while a high percentage of Boomers have experienced divorce, the majority of them are married today. Most Boomers value fidelity, even if experienced as serial monogamy. Consequently, a significant number of married Boomers find themselves as heads of blended families where it is not unusual to have household members with several different surnames. Both Gen X and the Millennial Generation have been significantly impacted and shaped by these changes in many American families. Seeing and feeling the failure of their parents' marriage, many in these younger generations are hesitant to make relational commitments. A major challenge for local churches today is to know how to effectively minister, not only to them, but also to blended, single parent, multigenerational, and other types of nontraditional families.

While Boomers were the first generation to use and abuse drugs in large numbers, today they are the generation leading the anti-drug, anti-smoking, and anti-drinking campaigns. Many Boomers have even become moralistic in their views of how other people should live and act. It was Boomers who popularized self-help groups as the means to personal transformation. From the health club to anti-addiction groups to family counseling, Boomers believe no problem is too big for treatment. Many churches have catered to Boomers' therapeutic culture by offering a wide variety of self-help and recovery groups.

One value that the Boomers retained from previous generations was the importance of work. However, differing from the GI and Silent Generations, Boomers have not worked and will not work at just *any* job. Instead, they expect their work to be meaningful, fulfilling, and significant. Boomers will often change careers and jobs when their work does not meet these criteria. Because this idealistic view of work is often not met in the real world, many Boomers experience frustration and unfulfillment in their work lives. Most Boomers today are employed and plan to keep working even as they reach traditional retirement ages; they do not necessarily want to retire and, in many cases, cannot afford to retire.

Unlike preceding generations, most Boomers are not good savers. They like to spend. In fact, Boomers are still the dominant consumers of products and services. Since members of the Boomer Generation have always seen themselves as unique, they do not take well to one-size-fits-all products and services. Instead, they like to buy distinctive products and do unique things. Many new products and services have been created to satiate the consumer appetite of the Boomer Generation. For example, Boomers, especially the Generation Jonesers, drove up the market for minivans and SUVs until gas prices soared, and they will probably drive the market for hybrid cars and other alternative vehicles.

Having fun is also important to Boomers. They have fueled the market in grown up toys such as sport cars, sailboats, quality golf clubs, mountain bikes, and other expensive recreational products. The toy trend started by the Boomers has continued in Gen X and in the Millennial Generation. Humor has also been an important value to the Boomer Generation and it remains so today. It was Boomer comedians, such as Robin Williams, Steve Martin, John Belushi, and the Saturday Night Live crew that stretched the boundary of acceptable humor.

Even as they age, many do not want to change their lifestyle. Boomers will continue to see their generation as the center of social change. Partially because of their size and partially because of their attitudes, Boomers have been successful at bringing consumerism to many areas of American life. For example, healthcare was not a consumer issue until Boomers came along. They have also taken quickly to changes in technology, especially in the use of cell phones, pocket PCs, BlackBerrys, computers, the Internet and various other forms of evolving technologies. Also, as more Boomers become empty nesters, they will eat out and travel more.

However one feels about the Boomer Generation, they will continue to be a major force in America for decades to come. Churches need to contend with aging Boomers if they are to remain vital and effective.

Boomer Spirituality

The Boomer Generation brought spirituality out of the closet. Both the GI and Silent Generations primarily see spirituality as personal and private. By contrast, Boomers have made the pursuit of spiritual meaning a lifelong avocation, especially as they move into midlife and older adulthood. In his book, *Spiritual Marketplace: Baby Boomers and the Remaking of American Religion,* Wade Clark Roof writes, "some aging Baby Boomers sense a need for that which transcends themselves and gives meaning and purpose to their lives and are able to articulate that need very clearly. Already deeply touched by a post-1960s psychological culture, now in midlife they seem to be searching further, in a more mature and focused manner."[3]

For the Boomer Generation, the quest for spiritual understanding has often been less than orthodox. In fact, their spirituality is usually of the mix-and-match variety, even among churchgoers. In their book *Generations: The History of America's Future, 1584-2069,* William Strauss and Neil Howe credit the Boomer Generation with initiating an "awakening" in the 1960s that was an intense and passionate time of spiritual searching and upheaval. Alternative forms of spirituality ushered in during this time are now commonplace in American society, even among professing Christians. Because many young Boomers were suspicious of institutional religion, they sought spiritual reality in the drug culture, Eastern mystical religions, astrology and other nonorthodox experiences. Often Boomers would blend alternative spirituality with orthodox Christian teachings, and many still do so today.

Significant numbers of Boomers are still ambivalent toward institutional religion. Many believe that they can be spiritual without being religious and Boomers are the first generation to make this distinction. In the book, *A Generation of Seekers: The Spiritual Journeys of the Baby Boom Generation*, Wade Clark Roof and others interviewed hundreds of Boomers and found a shift in religious vocabulary: "Almost all of the people we talked to had an opinion about the differences between being 'religious' and being 'spiritual.' While they did not always agree as to what the difference was, they were sure there was one."[4] Church leaders usually do not understand this distinction very well. Consequently, many are confused and appalled when they learn that many congregation members are more knowledgeable about their horoscope than they are about the Bible. One of the greatest challenges church leaders face today is to communicate the gospel in ways that make sense to a spiritually eclectic generation of Boomers.

Also in the book *A Generation of Seekers,* Roof and his team recorded the results of many surveys and interviews of Boomers that give some insights into their spiritual lives. They identified several groups of Boomers and how they relate to spirituality and Christianity. The first group is the "nonreligious" who have little or no interest in spirituality or church. The second group is the "dropouts" who once attended church but rarely do so now. The authors called the third group the "returnees." This group of Boomers once attended church, perhaps as children, and have returned to church because of a renewed interest in spiritual matters. The final group identified by the surveys and interviews are the "loyalists." These Boomers never left the church and have a relatively high loyalty to a denomination or local church.

As Boomers age, their spiritual journeys may intensify. A major challenge for local churches will be to actively engage Boomers in a growing faith. Since most Boomers are used to consuming goods and services, they often approach churches as consumers. A major challenge for ministry leaders will be to teach Boomers that a vital faith in Jesus Christ is more than just another alternative to meeting their felt needs. Instead, they will need to communicate the biblical message that being a follower of Jesus is a 24-7 commitment and lifestyle. If Boomers want significance, this is significance!

Chapter 6
Generation X

Most of the young adults in America today are members of Generation X, or Gen X. This generation was born between 1963 and 1981 and numbers about 56 million. (The population figures for Gen X vary widely because so many different time periods are used to define this generation.) This group probably received its name from Douglas Coupland's 1991 novel *Generation X: Tales for an Accelerated Culture*. The book is the fictional story of twenty-somethings Andy, Claire, and Dag and their aimless search for change and meaning in the California desert. Faced with the prospects of meaningless lives and a series of McJobs, the trio creates troubling, but humorous, tales about nuclear waste, overdosing, and the American mall culture. As the story continues, a dark side to this emerging generation reveals a powerful anxiety about their future and the uneasy difficulty of trying to move on to adulthood. While in many ways these literary images have stereotyped Generation X, the members of this generation are more complex than Coupland's portrayal. Although members of Gen X have balked at being labeled by any name, they are stuck with other tags as well: Baby Busters, 13th Generation, the Computer Generation, Slackers, and a variety of other monikers.

Peter Menconi

Gen X Life Events

The Gen Xers' formative years produced a wide variety of life events that helped shape their values and worldview. In the early 1970s when the oldest Gen Xers were moving through their elementary school years and into adolescence, America was not a very happy place. As the nation emerged from the turbulent 1960s, Americans were still wrestling with the impact of the Vietnam War. The Watergate scandal was unfolding. The subsequent resignation of President Richard Nixon in 1974 only helped to fuel the Gen X perception that the world was a chaotic place. The Vietnam War, Watergate, and other traumas played a major role in shaping the attitudes of distrust and disinterest that many Gen Xers have toward government, politics, and politicians. A lingering political cynicism still exists today among many Gen Xers. (Members of this generation vote far less than proceeding generations and probably will go to the polls less than the Millennials who follow.)

When Jimmy Carter became president in 1976, the United States was entering a long period of economic stagnation. Loss of jobs, an energy crisis, oil embargos, and other negative economic events helped to make the 1970s a dismal time for older Gen Xers. By the end of the decade the inflation rate hit 13.5 percent and the prime rate would reach 21 percent. Many families struggled under the weight of these burdens. The lunacy of the decade continued when in late November 1978, many young Gen Xers and their families were shocked by TV reports of a mass suicide at Jonestown, Guyana. In an inexplicable act of mass destruction, Jim Jones, the self-proclaimed leader of a cult known as the Peoples Temple, ordered more than 900 of his followers to drink a Kool-Aid and cyanide concoction. In addition, the latter part of the 1970s saw the fall of the Shah of Iran and the rise of Ayatollah Khomeini and Islamic fundamentalism to power. In 1979 America and President Carter were humiliated when fundamentalists took U.S. embassy workers in Tehran as hostages. These events foreshadowed the future conflict and confrontation Americans would have with Islamic militants. As Gen Xers grew, even sports were not immune from international violence and intrigue. The 1972 Olympics in Munich, Germany saw the massacre of 11 Israeli athletes by Arab terrorists. And in response to the Soviet invasion of Afghanistan, the United States boycotted the 1980 Summer Olympics held in Moscow and the Russians returned the favor when they boycotted the 1984 Los Angeles Summer Olympics.

Gen Xers learned a lesson in environmental pollution when the worst nuclear accident in the United States occurred in 1979 at Three Mile Island in Pennsylvania. The environmental sensitivities of Gen X were challenged many more times as they came of age. In 1986, the world's worst nuclear disaster occurred in Chernobyl, Ukraine, U.S.S.R., causing widespread radioactive contamination. Then in 1989, the tanker Exxon Valdez spilled more than a million barrels of crude oil into Prince Williams Sound in Alaska. TV images of dead birds and sea otters saturated with oil have left an indelible impression on the minds and hearts of many Gen Xers. Add the discovery of a hole in the ozone layer and many Xers were left to wonder about the fate of our planet.

While older Gen Xers were affected by the life events of the 1970s, generally speaking, this generation was most impacted by the events of the 1980s which began with the inauguration of Ronald Reagan as the 40th American president and the release of the embassy hostages in Iran. The remarkable decade of the 1980s ended with the toppling of the Berlin Wall. In between, many varied life events helped shape Gen Xers into who they are today. President Reagan was shot in 1981, once again reminding Gen Xers that the world can be a dangerous place. The equalitarian, multicultural, multiethnic attitudes of Gen Xers were reinforced by the appointment of Sandra Day O'Conner as the first female Supreme Court justice and the candidacy of Jesse Jackson for the presidency. At the same time, Gen X was becoming less white and more multiracial. Most Gen Xers, especially those who grew up in urban areas, are more comfortable with a diverse society than are the generations that preceded them.

Any distrust Gen Xers had toward people in authority was further reinforced by the Iran Contra investigation. To boot, presidential hopeful Gary Hart's electability ended with the disclosure of his sexual liaisons with Donna Rice. Christianity also took a hit in credibility when televangelist Jim Bakker admitted to sexual infidelity and Jimmy Swaggert resigned over his admission of frequent rendezvous with prostitutes. Even the Pope was under attack as a Turkish assailant attempted to assassinate him in 1981.

While national and global turmoil during their formative years did not help Gen Xers feel secure, changes on the home front created the most upheaval. In 1970, California became the first state to adopt a no-fault divorce law. The trend spread across America—the divorce rate spiraled upward. The way our society viewed children also began to change. In 1973, the U.S. Supreme Court overturned anti-abortion laws sending Gen Xers the message that they were an unwanted generation. (Generation X is a smaller generation than the generations that precede and follow them, due in part to legalized abortion.) During this time, the methods of having children also changed. For example, the first "test-tube baby" was born in Oldham, England on July 25, 1978 amid intense controversy over the safety and morality of the procedure. In 1983, the first surrogate baby was born. Gen X also saw major changes in the ways our society defined a family. As households broke up and reassembled in different ways, a *family* was redefined. In addition to traditional two-parent families, we now talk about single-parent families, blended and step families, multiple-generation families, joint custody families, and so on.

Perhaps the single most important event in the lives of many Gen Xers was the divorce of their parents, experienced by over 40 percent of Gen Xers. The negative impact of divorce upon these children has been documented widely. In their book *The Unexpected Legacy Of Divorce*, authors Judith S. Wallerstein, Julia M. Lewis, and Sandra Blakeslee summarize the results of their study on the long-term impact of divorce on children. Judith Wallerstein began her research in 1971 with interviews of 131 children of divorced families in Marin County. She followed up with the children over the years and, at the 25-year mark, compared their experiences with those of their peers whose parents had stayed together.

Among the research findings presented in the book, a few are particularly revealing:

- Only 60% of the adult children of divorce were married, compared with 80% of adults whose parents stayed married.

- The children of divorce were far more likely to marry before age 25, (50% compared with 11% of the comparison group). In the children of divorce group 57% of the early marriages failed compared with 25% of early marriages in the other group.

- While 38 % of adult children of divorce have their own children, 17% of the children were out of wedlock. In the comparison group, 61 percent have children, all in the context of marriage.

- Only 29% of children from divorced families received consistent support for higher education from their fathers, compared with 88% of the children from intact families.

- Fully 25% of children of divorce used drugs and alcohol before age fourteen compared with 9% of the comparison group.[1]

Gen Xers' school experiences were often chaotic. Throughout their school years, Gen Xers were often educational guinea pigs, as Silent and Boomer educators tried the latest educational fad on their unexpecting students. Open classrooms versus closed classrooms created an ongoing debate, as Gen Xers were caught in the crossfire over the value and harm of open classrooms. Values clarification and diversity curricula began to appear regularly in lesson plans. Many latchkey Gen Xers returned from school to an empty house with no parent to encourage and assist them in their school work. Often TV became the electronic baby-sitter that filled the time until a parent returned from work.

It is not surprising that Gen Xers' test scores plum-meted. (For example, Gen X SAT scores were significantly lower than those of the preceding Boomers and the Mil-lennials who followed.) Waves of criticism from educators and other observers gave the nation the picture that this generation was a group of underachievers. A smaller per-centage of Gen Xers went to and finished college than did Boomers. (Millennials will also probably attend college at a higher rate than Gen Xers.) While their educational short-comings may add to Gen Xers' angst, many do not accept the notion that they are a "dumb and dumber" generation. Many Xers believe that the way people learn has changed, which in fact, appears to be the case. Today, we can access most any type of information we want or need in minutes, if not seconds. And many Gen Xers know how to put this information to practical use. As they move through adult-hood, it will be interesting to see how Gen Xers use their hard learned survival instincts and skills to impact their lives and the lives of others.

The 1980s held other life events that helped to shape the world of coming-of-age Gen Xers. In 1981, a mysteri-ous disease began to take the lives of homosexual men. Later named the Acquired Immune Deficiency Syndrome, or AIDS, the disease began to affect and change the sex-ual behavior of many Gen Xers. The sexual revolution, as started and known by Boomers, was ending. The first ar-

93

tificial heart transplant procedure in 1982 foreshadowed the amazing medical research and treatments that were to follow. Additional technology and technological innovations rapidly began to transform our lives. With the development of the microprocessors, Apple computers and IBM PCs rolled off the lines. The introduction of personal computers fueled the astounding technological revolution that would greatly impact the lives of Gen Xers and the rest of us. Gen Xers readily took to these new technological tools and toys.

Television, the playground of the three major networks, also began to radically change. CNN was launched as the first all-news network and MTV was born as a 24-hour music station. In 1983, compact discs were introduced, greatly changing the way we listen to music, while Pac-Man energized a video game craze that has not subsided to this day. The wide sale and use of video cameras changed the way we recorded life and invaded privacy and anonymity. America's Funniest Home Videos, a precursor to reality TV, used the video camera to poke fun at all of us. Getting laughs at the expense of others has become a common Gen X trait. Today, reality TV has brought this entertainment-at-the-expense-of-others to a new level.

Columbia, the first space shuttle, was launched in 1981 and the new frontier seemed conquerable. Then, one of the most traumatic events in the lives of Gen Xers occurred when technology failed. On January 28, 1986, the space shuttle Challenger exploded in a ball of fire shortly after takeoff, killing all seven astronauts on board. To this day, many Gen Xers can tell you where they were and what they were doing when they heard the news of the space shuttle's demise. Challenger's explosion parallels the assassination of JFK for Boomers as a most-memorable life event for many Gen Xers. While not presenting the same national and international trauma as a president's death, the Challenger disaster underscored the fallibility of technology and the uncertainty of life for Gen Xers.

A series of political and economic events in the late 1980s led to the dismantling of the Berlin Wall, an enduring symbol of the Cold War that pitted the West, mainly the United States, against the East, primarily the Soviet Union. The fall of the Berlin Wall was soon followed by the disintegration of the Soviet Union, and nations that had been overrun by Communists during and after World War II began to reemerge. Old ethnic tensions also reemerged, and many people who had never known freedom struggled with change. Gen Xers inherited a whole new world.

Gen X Popular Culture

The importance of popular culture in the lives of Gen Xers is pervasive. As we have seen, a significant number of Xers were latchkey kids who came home to an empty house where the television was the electronic babysitter. In his book *Virtual Faith: The Irreverent Spiritual Quest of Generation X*, Tom Beaudoin writes about this experience:

> The latchkey childhood of my generational peers was central in establishing our deep relationship with pop culture—largely through the media. In loco parentis, television provided daily entertainment for those who had to fill time between the end of the school day and the return of working parents. My generation later reported that we spent more

time with the television than with our parents during childhood.[2]

If you want to understand Gen Xers, begin by learning about their attachment to pop culture and its tremendous influence on their lives. Pop culture's impact on the oldest Gen Xers was first felt in the mid-1970s. As budding adolescents they were introduced to the fads of pet rocks and mood rings. Video recorders and players opened a whole new dimension of home entertainment. Childhood movie favorites such as *Jaws*, *Rocky*, and *Star Wars* could now be enjoyed at home. The youngest Gen Xers entertained themselves with *Sesame Street* and the *Muppets*, while older siblings were engrossed with Smurfs and Cabbage Patch dolls. The mention of Rubik's Cube and Transformers today will trigger animated conversations and bring fond memories to many Gen Xers. Many young women can remember the fun they had mimicking a Valley Girl and mastering VALspeak. "Gag me with a spoon…TOTALLY."

Television was the major pop cultural influence in Gen Xers' lives. For example, the Brady Bunch was the family many Gen Xers longed for. Young Gen Xers were fascinated by the 1977 miniseries *Roots* that traced the family history of Kunta Kinte, a West African youth who became a slave in America. Eighty million Americans watched this realistic portrayal of the black-American experience, helping to shape the attitudes of a generation. Many Gen Xers, both black and white, knew little of the struggles of the civil rights movement and the convulsions it created in America. Consequently, *Roots* provided a profound educational experience for a whole generation. It can be argued that some of the roots of the egalitarian attitudes of Generation X can be traced to this miniseries.

The last episode of M*A*S*H aired in 1983, signaling the end of the Boomers dominance of TV. As cable television entered its adolescence, Gen Xers became the target of TV moguls. Between 1981 and 1985, a new wave of cable networks gave many Americans a wider variety of programming options. Now Gen Xers had more choices to add to their pop culture repertoire. Multiple options have always been, and continue to be, important to Gen Xers. As many Xers were coming of age they could now watch The Disney Channel, Lifetime, MTV, The Weather Channel, Discovery Channel, Home Shopping Network, the Nashville Network, Arts & Entertainment, American Movie Classics, regional sports channels, and pay per view channels. By 1985, 6,600 cable systems served more than 41.5 million households. Gen Xers could now get serious about pop culture.

Despite the intrusion of this new phenomenon called cable TV, the three major networks would not go quietly. In 1984 NBC introduced *The Cosby Show,* a sit-com about the everyday lives of an upper-middle-class black family named the Huxtables. Cliff Huxtable, the father, was a respected gynecologist whose wife was a successful attorney. *The Cosby Show* was one of the biggest surprise hits in American television history and dominated Thursday evenings from 1984 to 1992. Despite its huge success, *The Cosby Show* was not without its critics. When *TV Guide* compared the Huxtables' lifestyle to other black families in America, it described them as "atypical." For other observers, *The Cosby Show* was a classy sitcom that humorously broke down many stereotypes white Americans had of African-Americans.

This show and an increasingly diverse pop culture helped to lay the groundwork for Generation X's view of America and the world as multiracial, multiethnic, and quite diverse. To a great extent pop culture's influence has brought Gen X to see the world from a more tolerant point of view than preceding generations. That is, Gen Xers are less likely to define others through racial and ethnic differences. They are more accepting of gender equality and less critical of alternative sexual lifestyles. These Gen X attitudes also have a profound effect on how they view the church. Many Gen Xers see local churches as homogeneous groups that do not accurately reflect the diverse society in which they live. Consequently, many Gen Xers see churches and churchgoers as narrow-minded and irrelevant.

Another example of the impact of television on the changing world of Gen Xers came in 1986 when Oprah Winfrey took her program national. Since then, Oprah (who is a Boomer) has been a major influence in shaping the values and worldview of millions in the United States and around the world. Since it aired nationwide, the show has remained the number one talk show on television. Oprah was included in *Time* magazine's "100 Most Influential People of the 20th Century." The *Time* article on Oprah states:

> "When Winfrey talks, her viewers listen. Any book she chooses for her on-air book club becomes an instant best seller. When she established the 'world's largest piggy bank,' people all over the country contributed spare change to raise more than $1 million (matched by Oprah) to send disadvantaged kids to

college. When she blurted that hearing about the threat of mad cow disease 'just stopped me cold from eating another burger!', the perceived threat to the beef industry was enough to trigger a multi-million-dollar lawsuit (which she won)."[3]

Needless to say, Oprah's influence is impressive. And while her message is primarily targeted to Boomers, she also helped shape the postmodern world of Gen Xers.

The postmodern influence of TV on Gen Xers also appeared in other programs. Starting in 1989, *Seinfeld* was a sitcom about "nothing" that made Gen Xers laugh. Jerry and his friends presented the worldview that life is aimless and needs to be taken one moment at a time. *The Simpsons* hit the airwaves in 1990 and Gen Xers loved it. But Bart and his family quickly came under criticism from parents, educators, politicians, the clergy, and others. Actually, the long-running animated series has shown itself to be both family-friendly and religion-respecting and continues to be a favorite among Xers and other generations. In his book *The Gospel According to The Simpsons,* Mark I. Pinsky writes:

> "*The Simpsons* is one of the most important common experiences in the American home," said Stewart Hoover, a religion and media scholar at the University of Colorado. In a study funded by the Lilly Foundation, Hoover found that "*The Simpsons* consistently comes up in our interviews as a subject for family discussion and interaction around issues of values and morality and religion. It's kind of a meeting place for families. The show has quite a cross-generational appeal and effect," he told me.[4]

Numerous writers and scholars have discussed and debated about the portrayal of religion in *The Simpsons*. While religion, like many other aspects of American society, is the target of the show's satire, it is given backhanded respect. Matt Groening, the creator of *The Simpsons*, expressed his perspective in an interview:

> What I think is funny about the antagonism that The Simpsons seems to inspire in some critics is that the storytelling is good, and to me that's what's good for kids, not moral exhortations to straighten your posture. But you know that there are all these little unspoken rules on TV: Characters can't smoke; everyone has to wear their seatbelt; drinking is frowned upon. And on The Simpsons, of course, our characters drink and smoke, don't wear seatbelts, and litter. On the other hand, right-wingers complain there's no God and religion on TV. Not only do the Simpsons go to church every Sunday and pray, they actually speak to God from time to time. We show him, and God has five fingers. Unlike the Simpsons, who only have four.[5]

Obviously, this is not your father's old-time religion. The opportunity to see the church and religion in America being satirized on TV is very appealing and funny for many Gen Xers.

More to the point, the portrayal of Christians and Christianity in *The Simpsons* is noteworthy. Pinsky goes on to write that "On American college and high school campuses today, the name most associated with the word "Christian"—other than Jesus—is not the pope or Mother

Teresa or even Billy Graham. Instead, it's a goofy-looking guy named Ned Flanders. Homer Simpson's next-door neighbor is the evangelical known most intimately to nonevangelicals."[6] While Ned Flanders absorbs his share of scorn and abuse on the show, he is not an unsympathetic figure. Pinsky writes that "Ned's faith is constant, and in the end it is always affirmed. Yet like most Christians, his faith is not perfect: God's will sometimes baffles him."[7] In an increasingly postmodern society, shows like *The Simpsons* are shaping the views of Gen Xers and Millennials toward religion in general and Christianity specifically. *The Simpsons* have had their long run on the FOX Network. Along with MTV, FOX has been the primary network of Generation X with groundbreaking shows such as *The Simpsons*, *Ally McBeal, Married with Children, Beverly Hills, 90210, X-Files, American Idol*, and others that changed TV programming and viewing. While FOX has been a lightening rod for criticism over the years, the criticism has been uneven. For example, while FOX's programming has been criticized for pushing the boundaries of TV too far, the FOX News Channel is often criticized for being too conservative. Perhaps this schizophrenia is indicative of the postmodern way that Gen X views the world.

In response to changing demographics, the three major networks attempted to appeal to the Gen X audience with programs such as *Friends, Survivor, Fear Factor, The Mole, Extreme Makeover*, and other shows. Influenced by the values and interests of Generation X, so-called 'reality' shows, such as *American Idol*, have become a steady staple on American TV. Even the cable channels have gotten into the act. Reality shows allow viewers to have vicarious experiences which is a major part of the Gen X lifestyle.

The influence of pop culture on Gen Xers is not limited to TV. Movies also have the eyes, ears, and attention of Xers. Movies such *as ET, Star Wars, Jaws, Rocky, Close Encounters of the Third Kind,* and *Raiders of the Lost Ark* added new expressions to our language: "ET phone home." "May the Force be with you." "Just when you thought it was safe to go into the water." But it was the movies of the 1980s that helped define this generation. For example, *The Breakfast Club* told the story of five teenagers who are assigned to Saturday detention. The group is made up of a jock, a hood, a rich girl, a geek, and an emotional basket case. As they talked about their lives, many high school Gen Xers in the movie audience could identify with them. The movie is an excellent example of what it was like to be a teenager in the mid-1980s. Other memorable 1980s movies for Gen Xers were less serious. *Ferris Bueller's Day Off* humorously portrayed the anti-authority and anti-institutional feelings of many Gen Xers. Teenaged Ferris Bueller (played by Matthew Broderick) cut school and set off on numerous adventures throughout Chicago and environs. While the movie had plenty of satire and comedy, it also made some serious points about status seeking and parental indifference, themes that hit home with many Gen Xers. Other movies such as *Footloose* and *Risky Business* also addressed the issues of intergenerational and subcultural tension and conflict. On a lighter note, *Bill and Ted's Excellent Adventure* was a comical portrayal of Gen X revisionist history and *Top Gun* gave Gen Xers "the need for speed."

Music was and is a major pop cultural influence in the lives of most Gen Xers as well. MTV began airing in 1981 and helped make the late Michael Jackson's *Thriller* the largest selling album, up to that time. His video *Thriller* also helped to launch the music video as a popular addition to the entertainment industry. Certainly the 1980s were a time of excess in the music industry. Ozzy Osbourne bit off the head of a bat thrown to him during a concert. With the release of her first album in 1983, Madonna had a significant impact on Gen Xers. Her brash lifestyle and ability to reinvent herself allowed her to be a trendsetter throughout the formative years of many Gen Xers. While perennial artists such as The Rolling Stones, Billy Joel, Bob Seger and the Silver Bullet Band, Fleetwood Mac, and Elton John continued to record in the 1980s, new artists and groups emerged. Most Gen Xers today can talk for hours about their favorite artists or groups and the music that marked their coming of age. Music and its messages continue to occupy an important place in the world of Xers.

Finally, if you are a member of Generation X, you may want to see how much of the following pop cultural trivia you remember from the 1980s:

Are You a Child of the 80s?

Trapped between the "Baby Boomers" and "Generation Y" is a special generation...a generation we call "Children of the Eighties." If you can identify with most of the 15 points below, chances are you are definitely one of them...

1. You owned a "real" Rubik's cube.
2. One word: Izod.
3. You remember when MTV didn't exist. Alternatively you remember when the M stood for Music, not Mundane.

4. "Alternative" music actually was—and not popular Top 40 tunes.
5. You were a "wanna be:" Madonna, Duran Duran, Michael Jackson, Cyndi Lauper, Boy George, etc.
6. "Where's the beef?"
7. You know how to use a rotary phone.
8. Max Headroom was cool.
9. You know how (or wanted to be able) to Moon-walk!
10. Atari, IntelliVision, TelStar and Coleco were the ultimate gaming systems to own.
11. Leg warmers and headbands a lá Pat Benatar once looked really cool to you.
12. You remember when Jordache jeans with a flat-handle comb in the back pocket were cool.
13. Jelly bracelets & shoes!
14. Your hair defied gravity.
15. You are still baffled by the "day glo" clothing trend. Source: www.80s.com/ChildrenOfTheEighties

Gen X Values and Worldviews

Generation X is the first truly postmodern generation. While 'postmodern' and 'postmodernism' are somewhat overused and poorly understood terms, they help separate Gen X worldviews from those of preceding generations. Postmodernism is a worldview that looks for nontraditional ways of processing information and interacting with the world. Primarily, postmodernism has brought Gen Xers to view reality as relative. That is, they do not readily accept the concept of absolute truth. In their book *Rocking the Ages*, J. Walker Smith and Ann Clurman write about the Gen X perspective: "No one thing is inherently good or bad—all things are potential options and the trade-offs have to be weighed and balanced. Each person must find an option that works for him or her own individual situation. If those choices work, then they're okay—respect and accept those choices, don't judge them or condemn them."[8] For many Gen Xers the standard for measuring what is true and good is usually one's individual experience. Needless to say, this aspect of a postmodern worldview has profound effects upon on how Christianity is viewed, accepted, or rejected.

While a precise definition of postmodernism is elusive, it can still be understood. One way of understanding postmodernism is to contrast it with modernism. The following summary contrasts the characteristics of modernism with postmodernism:

Modernism	Postmodernism
Specialized thinking	Holistic thinking
Convergent thinking	Divergent thinking
Linear worldview	Three-dimensional worldview
Absolute truth	Paradox/relativism
Logic	Intuition/ Experiences
Individualism	Community
National	Global/pluralism
Mass production	Customization
Scientific	Spiritual
Consumerism	Environmentalism
Monocultural	Multicultural
Concern for the powerful	Concern for the powerless
Propositional theology	Incarnational theology

As mentioned previously, perhaps the greatest factor and influence in shaping the values and worldview of many Gen Xers has been the divorce of their parents, as 40 to 45 percent of Gen Xers are children of divorce. (Between 1965 and 1979 the divorce rate jumped 130 percent.) Even Xers whose parents did not divorce were impacted by the high divorce rate among their peers' parents. In his book *Jesus for a New Generation: Putting the Gospel in the Language of Xers*, Kevin Graham Ford writes:

> Many of us had parents who divorced, who had affairs, who dragged us through a series of unhappy, short-lived marriages or who walked out on us. "I come from a family of divorce, like half my generation," said a young man in one of my focus groups. "I wish my childhood had been happier, but it's something I just need to accept. I hope my generation will be able to make some different choices and that life won't be as unhappy for the next generation." The emotional residue of these dysfunctional family experiences hover over my generation like a storm cloud: anger, alienation, frustration, and low self-esteem.[9]

Some have offered that the dysfunctional family experiences of many Gen Xers have left them with post-traumatic stress disorder (PTSD). In their book *A Generation Alone: Xers Making a Place in the World,* William Mahedy and Janet Bernardi write:

> Generation X, the next generation after the Vietnam era, suffers from a double affliction: a great many

of them have been traumatized in ways that cause PTSD (abuse, violence, and so forth); but, more significantly, most of them are stressed out simply by living under current social conditions. The present social disorder is so great that simply being young today is a stressor for a huge segment of the twentysomething generation. I can find no other explanation for the widespread problems with stability, self-image, feelings of emptiness, depression, suicidal thinking, fear of the future and lack of hope among the young.[10]

These words were written more than ten years ago and twentysomethings are now at least thirtysomethings. While some have experienced healing, others continue to live with the residual effects of unstable childhoods.

As a response to the lack of healthy childhood relationships, many Gen Xers long for community and authentic friendships. Mahedy and Bernardi write, "In a culture like ours, where the individual is so dehumanized, the recovery of genuine humanity begins with the forming of real friendships. Friends genuinely care for one another. A friend does not 'use' the other person to achieve some goal—for example, befriending only those coworkers who enhance one's chances of a promotion. Friends trust each other. For Xers who have learned not to trust anyone, friendship is a decisive step in the direction of healing."[11] It is not coincidental that the TV show *Friends* was a big hit for so many years. Many Gen X viewers longed to be in a community of friends like the one depicted on the TV screen.

The childhood and adolescent experiences of many Gen Xers have shaped their attitudes toward marriage and parenting. A 2001 Gallop poll commissioned by the National Marriage Project of Rutgers University uncovered some interesting Gen X attitudes in never-married singles in the 20 to 29 age range:

- 78% of the Gen Xers agreed that a couple should not get married unless they are prepared to stay together for life.
- 45% of the respondents agreed that the government should not even be involved in licensing marriage.
- 43% of the Gen Xers agreed that the government should provide cohabitating couples with the same benefits as married couples.
- 16% of the young adults agreed that the main purpose of marriage is to raise children.
- More than 40% of the 20 to 29 year olds agreed that adults who intentionally raise a child out of wedlock are simply "doing their own thing."
- 40% of single women agreed with the statement, "although it might not be the ideal option, you would consider having a child on your own if you reached your mid-thirties and had not found the right man to marry."[12]

Similar attitudes are reflected in a book by Pamela Paul called *The Starter Marriage and the Future of Matrimony*. Paul interviewed 60 young divorced men and women with some interesting insights. She claims that Gen Xers are getting married, trying it out, and getting divorced before they have children. Paul calls these "starter marriages" that end for a variety of reasons: "Starter marriages, like all marriages, are meant to last forever. But they don't. Instead, they fizzle out within five years, always ending before children begin."[13] Starter marriages are rampant in pop culture as movie, TV, and pop music stars almost accept them as the norm.

Needless to say, the attitudes and actions of many Gen Xers toward marriage and parenthood are quite different from previous generations. Despite these attitudes and actions, Gen Xers still hold marriage and parenthood in high regard. Most want a successful marriage and desire to raise a healthy family. But most do not want the marriage of their parents. They don't see themselves as permissive and nondirective mothers and fathers like their parents were. Unfortunately, many Gen Xers are poorly equipped to handle the intensity of relationship that marriage and parenting demand. It is ironic that the Gen X quest for intimacy, community, and authentic friendships is so elusive. Past relational wounds keep many Gen Xers from making long-term commitments to relationships. In his book *In Search of Authentic Faith: How Emerging Generations are Transforming the Church*, Steve Rabey writes, "Talking about community and creating it are two different things, and there are indications that the brokenness and alienation that many young people have experienced makes them more hungry for community but also may make them less able to create it and sustain it."[14]

Despite their desire for healthy relationships, many Gen Xers have a difficult time making commitments to lasting relationships, especially in marriage. In his book, *The Power of Commitment: A Guide to Active, Lifelong Love*, Dr. Scott Stanley writes, "As divorce has become far more common, the level of confidence that people have in marriage has gone down. This is widely believed by researchers to be the reason that young people are putting off marriage until an older and older age, that they are more likely than ever before to have children without being married, that they feel they must be financially established prior to marrying, and that they enter into prenuptial agreements. People are hedging their bets because after all, you can't be too sure about marriage anymore—or so these people believe."[15]

While a number of observers have suggested that Gen Xers form tribes or committed groups of relationships, these groups usually end up being transient and self-serving. When Gen Xers do move into marriage, it is often with some reluctance and trepidation. And in marriage many Gen X couples remain childless or delay childbirth. It is not coincidental that the number of pets has skyrocketed in America over the past decade or so. (There are currently many more pets, especially dogs and cats in the United States than people.) Many Gen X couples consider their dogs or cats their babies, as pets take less long-term commitment than children.

There are other values and characteristics of Gen Xers that differ significantly from the generations that preceded them. For example, the demographics of Generation X are much more diverse than preceding generations. Most Gen Xers are more comfortable with ethnic and racial diversity than Silents and Boomers. In their book *Boomers, Xers, and other Strangers*, Rick and Kathy Hicks write, "One of the most significant characteristics that describes or identifies the Gen Xers is their commitment to diversity. They grew up in a time when various minority groups were gaining national attention and demanding rights. They have been sensitized to the variety of people and taught to recognize them as individuals worthy of respect and an increasing level of tolerance. They were not raised to value conformity, but diversity."[16]

Gen Xers egalitarian sensibilities level the playing field in the workplace and in most areas of life. They want to be treated as peers by others and not as subordinates or second-class citizens. In addition, Gen Xers do not wrestle with the gender gap as intensely as previous generations; the battle of the sexes has greatly diminished. Relatedly, Gen Xers are a diverse generation that values differences and uniqueness. As noted previously, Gen Xers are more ethnically and racially diverse and have a more expansive global worldview. While racism still exists in America, it is less of a factor among Gen Xers of different racial backgrounds. As the global village has become more of a reality for Xers, many of this generation see the world as their backyard and playground. It is not uncommon for Gen Xers to travel the world, often for no apparent reason except to have the experience and because they can.

Since most Gen Xers ascribe to a live-and-let-live philosophy, they are quite comfortable with diverse sexual lifestyles. They have lived with so much contradiction and paradox that they have few illusions left. When asking a question, it is not uncommon to get a response of "Whatever!" from a Gen Xer. Bruce Tulgan (a Gen Xer) gives us some insight into this generational perspective in his book *Managing Generation X.* He writes that "Growing up in an environment of rapid change and social atomization, without the backdrop of the 1950s and 1960s idealism, Xers

Peter Menconi

have had few opportunities to witness or experience en-during affiliations of any kind—social, geographical, reli-gious, or political."[17]

Another obvious difference between Gen Xers and the older generations is the popularity of tattoos and body piercing in the younger generation. While psychologists have offered a number of explanations why tattoos and body piercing have become more widespread, the reasons may be as varied as the tattoo designs that color the Gen Xers' skin. Some say they tattoo and/or pierce themselves for artistic and individualistic reasons. Others do it as a form of rebellion, self mutilization, peer pressure, and conformi-ty. Whatever the reason, these obvious outward trimmings have often driven a communication wedge between Gen Xers and older generations. Many GIs, Silents, and Boomers stereotype people who pierce and/or tattoo their bodies. (It remains to be seen if Millennials will continue this fad and make it a trend.)

Gen Xers have been encouraged and taught to work in teams throughout much of their educational experience. Generally speaking, many Gen Xers see collaboration and teamwork in life as more important than their predecessors. Consequently, many Gen Xers have an aversion to hierar-chical ways of getting things done. Bruce Tulgan explains it this way: "Too many managers think that when Xers com-plain about intermediate managers it is because we are arrogant and don't want to deal with anyone but the top managers. It is true that Xers resent answering to manag-ers whose only role is to fill another sphere of authority in the corporate hierarchy. Xers object to dealing with inter-mediate managers just as we object to dealing with other

112

obstacles to our creativity."[18] Gen Xers often see corporate structures and institutions as sterile and impersonal, and as a result, many don't do rules well. That is, they often go about their work and life pragmatically and practically, and, consequently, may bypass conventional methods.

The concept of balanced living is also extremely important to many Gen Xers. They strongly believe in balancing their work with the rest of their lives. They "work to live" not "live to work"—a criticism they often level at Boomers. Many Xers see Boomers as workaholics. In their life equation, playtime is quite important to Gen Xers. Time with friends, time in nature and the outdoors, time for excitement are just a few Gen X preferences. Many Gen Xers grew up as risk takers who involved themselves in exciting, exhilarating, and dangerous activities. They were the first skateboarders and snowboarders. Four-wheeling and motocross fit many Gen Xers needs for excitement, as do bungee jumping, hang gliding, rock climbing, and extreme and out-of-bounds skiing. The Summer and Winter X Games help satiate Xers "need for speed." Some of this risk- taking behavior stems from the Gen X philosophy: Since tomorrow is uncertain, live for today. In an article in *First Things*, writer Sarah E. Hinckley describes the uncertain world of Gen Xers: "We recognize this world: ripped from the start by our parents' divorces, spoiled by our own bad choices, threatened by war and poverty, pain and meaninglessness. Ours is a world where inconvenient lives are aborted and inconvenient loves are abandoned."[19]

Above all, Gen Xers are survivors. As latchkey children, many relied upon themselves, and still rely on themselves. Most Gen Xers are comfortable with change and are

Peter Menconi

quite good at it. Many have learned to be shrewd and readily know how to obtain what they want. Oftentimes their technological savvy gives them an edge in getting what they want, if not necessarily what they need. Other times, their shrewdness isolates them from the very relationships that would help bring healing in their lives. Wise church leaders and congregations can help Gen Xers arrive at a balance between independence and interdependence; survival and "thrival."

Gen X Spirituality

As we have already seen, Gen Xers' spirituality provides a formidable challenge for churches. Sarah Hinckley gives us an overview of this challenge:

> We've never been proud to be Americans—our political memory stretches back only as far as Vietnam, Watergate, and Reaganomics. Our parents left religion and, perhaps not coincidentally, each other in unprecedented numbers. Failed ideologies were mother's milk to us: love didn't save the world, the Age of Aquarius brought no peace, sexual liberation brought us AIDS and legions of fatherless children, Marxism collapsed. We can't even imagine a world of cultural or national unity; our world is more like a tattered patchwork quilt. We have every little inconsequential thing, Nintendo 64s and homepages and cell phones, but not one important thing to believe in. We are the much–maligned Generation X: your mission is to get us back to church.[20]

A study by the Barna Research Group confirms the absence of Gen Xers, especially twentysomethings, from the local church. The study states, "Perhaps the most striking reality of twentysomething's faith is their relative absence from Christian churches. Only 3 out of 10 twentysomethings (31%) attend church in a typical week, compared to 4 out of 10 of those in their 30s (42%) and nearly half of all adults age 40 and older (49%)."[21]

While Gen Xers are spiritual seekers, their search is significantly different from that of GIs, Silents, and Boomers. In many ways, Gen Xers are more serious about their spirituality, and they are, most certainly, more eclectic. In *Virtual Faith*, Tom Beaudoin gives us what he believes to be the major characteristics of Gen Xer's spiritual quest. He offers that Gen Xers are suspicious of and indifferent toward religious institutions; interested in individual and communal spiritual experiences; aware of the religious and spiritual significance of suffering; and wrestling with ambiguity. We get further insight into Gen X spirituality from Eddie Gibbs in his book *Church Next: Quantum Changes in How We Do Ministry*, "If boomers have customized the Christian faith, then their offspring have created their own religious beliefs. They have celebrated the diversity present in a pluralistic society that affirms toleration of other faiths and alternative lifestyles. The predominant mindset is, 'If your beliefs work for you, that's just fine!'"[22] Therefore, faith with no ultimate answers is attractive to many Xers; they are more comfortable with many religious, spiritual, and philosophical roads leading to a unifying truth. The tenet of absolute truth held by orthodox Christians throughout the centuries is foreign to many Gen Xers. Most Gen Xers do not see Christianity as the salvation of the world. While many are attracted to the person of Jesus Christ, they are cool to the practices and hypocrisy of local churches. In fact, many Xers see organized religions as major troublemakers in our world.

Nonetheless, Generation X wants a spiritual experience that is real and authentic. But where will they find it? To many Gen Xers the worship experience in Boomer churches is overproduced, contrived, and not appealing. They are often put off by cutting-edge productions and seeker-service manipulations that impress them as slick and insincere. Looking for alternatives many Gen Xers have allowed their soul searching to lead them into areas of mysticism and mystery. Consequently, churches are in competition with alternative forms of spiritual experience. Tom Beaudoin writes that "Xers did not invent this interest in paganism and mysticism; they learned it from their baby boomer elders. Generation Xers, however, are much more immersed now than boomers in experimentation, alienation, and pop-cultured religiousness, because we were steeped in pop culture, and on our own, at an earlier age."[23]

Examples of this eclectic spirituality and spiritual quest often appear on *Oprah*. Oprah has become a spiritual leader whose influence is addressed in an article titled "The Church of O" written by LaTonya Taylor. "Since 1994, when she abandoned traditional talk-show fare for more edifying content, and 1998, when she began "Change Your Life TV," Oprah's most significant role has become that of spiritual leader. To her audience of more than 22 million mostly female viewers, she has become a postmodern priestess—an icon of church-free spirituality. Indeed, much like a healthy church, Oprah creates community, provides information, and encourages people to evaluate and improve their lives."[24]

The article goes on to state, "as with a pastor and her parishioners, the bond between Oprah and those in her audience is sacred. She understands the magnitude of the power she wields over them and seems to want to use it to guide them toward better lives. But what does Oprah's appeal to so many Americans, particularly women, tell us about current American spirituality?" Taylor lists four major responses to this question:

- First, so-called secular Americans remain spiritually hungry.
- Second, Americans are interested in practical spirituality.
- Third, Americans yearn for a hopeful spirituality.
- Fourth, many Americans like to dabble in a variety of belief systems. Oprah summed up her approach to spirituality when she said, "One of the biggest mistakes humans make is to believe there is only one way. Actually, there are many diverse paths leading to what you call God."[25]

Such "cafeteria religion" is common today and not just among Gen Xers. In fact, it is important to recognize that similar views toward spirituality are held by a large percentage of the American population—even those who attend church most weekends. The results of another study by the Barna Research Group substantiated the presence of cafeteria religion:

> More than four out of five Americans claim to be Christian and half as many can be classified as born-again Christians. Nine out of ten adults own a Bible. Most adults read the Bible during the year and a huge majority claims they know all of the basic teachings of the Bible. How, then, can most people say Satan does not exist, that the Holy Spirit is merely a symbol, that eternal peace with God can be earned through good works, and that truth can only be understood through the lens of reason and experience? How can a plurality of our citizens contend that Jesus committed sins and that the Bible, Koran and Book of Mormon all teach the same truths?[26]

George Barna laments that "In a sound bite society you get sound bite theology. Americans are more likely to buy simple sayings than a system of truth that takes time and concentration to grasp. People are more prone to embrace diversity, tolerance and feeling good than judgment, discernment, righteousness and limitations. People are more focused on temporal security than eternal security and its temporal implications. Hopefully, once Christian leaders and teachers comprehend this we can be more devoted to effectively challenging the superficial spirituality of our nation."[27]

There are several other characteristics of Gen X spirituality that are important to understand. For many Xers the experiential journey is "the thing." That is, Gen Xers are far more interested in experiencing God at all levels of their lives than experiencing church or organized religion. Faith in God needs to be a passionate, healing, and transformational journey. Consequently, the experience of worship is a high priority for Xers. It is often an eclectic blend of premodern Christian liturgy, artistic and multisensory expression, and modern technological wizardry. Eddie Gibbs expresses it this way:

> This generation is one that responds to a multisensory message. Some of the churches reaching out to Gen Xers resemble the seeker-sensitive churches of the 1980s in some respects but even go beyond them in informality, a relational style of communication and an updated contemporary style of worship. In other respects they are very different. They combine ancient forms of worship with the modern, ranging in style from Gregorian chants to Hip Hop, and using icons, candles and incense as aids to worship, plus strobe lights and knee-high clouds!"[28]

But above all, worship for Gen Xers needs to be participative. Worship is to be experienced—there are no spectators.

Another characteristic of Gen X spirituality is that the journey with Jesus Christ needs to be incarnational and missional. A living faith that affects every area of life is to be put into action and taken to a broken world. Many Gen X Christians believe that an authentic faith is personally healing and transformational and at the same time, world-changing. Faith in Jesus Christ should have an impact on the problems and pain of people worldwide. Since Gen

Xers frequently identify with people in pain, they are often willing to minister to the homeless, the powerless, and the marginalized. Gen Xers will tutor and mentor disadvantaged youth; they will minister to gays and lesbians wrestling with HIV or their sexual identities; they will help provide shelter and food for the homeless; they will work to preserve the environment; and they will minister wherever they feel God calls them. Unfortunately, most local churches are not able to engage, challenge, and grow Gen Xers in these areas of their spiritual journey.

Gen X Needs

The woundedness that so many Xers have experienced means that most Gen Xers have an overwhelming need to find a place where they can heal, trust, grow, and flourish. In *Generating Hope: A Strategy for Reaching the Postmodern Generation*, Jimmy Long writes, "Their longing is for a place to belong, a place to call home. As we have already seen, Generation X is suffering from the effects of the dysfunctional family, which are causing them to search for new places to belong. The traditional family, because of its dysfunctionality has become a place many Xers feel they no longer belong. Influenced by the tribalism inherent in postmodernism, this generation, unlike other recent generations, is moving away from the individualism of the Enlightenment era and into the communal spirit of postmodernism."[29]

A similar observation is made by Hahn and Verhaagen in their book *GenXers After God* as they call the church to respond to this opportunity and challenge. "Generation X highly values relational interconnectedness, yet many members of the generation seem not to know how to re-late. The gospel calls us from our shattered relationships, estrangement, isolation, and abuse-filled backgrounds to the new, safe community of God's people, who have experienced Christ's graciously liberating love. The community is not utopian, because it is made up of sinful people, but it is at its best a taste of life in the already, the way it will be in the not yet."[30] While the local church holds the greatest hope of helping Gen Xers heal, it will be a difficult task. As we have seen, most Xers do not attend church and do not have a positive image of organized religion. Yet, as they age, Gen Xers may slowly return to churches they see have something to offer. When they come, local churches need to be ready.

Chapter 7
Millennial Generation

A new generation has arrived—they are the Millennials. Born between 1982 and 2000, the oldest members of this generation have graduated from high school and college and have entered the workplace. They were named Millennials by Howe and Strauss in their book *Generations* because they are the first generation to come of age in the new millennium. Other names given to this generation are Generation Y, Generation WHY, Generation Next, Echo Boom Generation, Mosaic Generation, Hip Hop Generation, Net Generation, 9/11 Generation, Generation D (for *digital*), Pepsi Generation, Bridger Generation, Choice Generation, and more. In typical Millennial Generation fashion, an Internet poll was conducted to name the generation after X. Through the process of elimination, the name Generation Y won out over Millennial Generation by a slim margin (see www.demochoice.org). We will use the name Millennial Generation here because it is more descriptive of this generation's place in history.

Many sociologists, marketers, and pop-culture watchers have already shifted their attention away from Boomers and Gen Xers to Millennials. There are more than 80 million members of the Millennial Generation, which makes them larger than the Boomer Generation. Their grandparents are usually from the Silent Generation and their parents are either Boomers or Gen Xers. The children of Millennials, along with the children of some Gen Xers, will comprise the new generation currently being born. New names will be attached to this youngest generation in the next few years.

Millennial Life Events

Members of the Millennial Generation started to arrive in the early 1980s. The oldest members of this generation barely remember Ronald Reagan, yet in their brief lifetime, America and the world have profoundly changed. Technological advances, globalization, urbanization, popular culture, and the redefinition of the family are just a few factors transforming the way the Millennial Generation looks at and lives life. In addition, major events such as the O.J. Simpson trial, Columbine shootings, Oklahoma City bombing, impeachment of President Clinton, Princess Diana's death, destruction of the World Trade Center on September 11, 2001, "dot bomb" fiasco, and wars in Iraq and Afghanistan have helped to shape Millennials' worldview. As with other generations, such events have taught Millennials that the world is a dangerous and unpredictable place. Due in part to these experiences many members of this generation have become pragmatic and self-reliant.

The impact of the Columbine killings and the events of 9/11 on Millennials are similar to the JFK assassination for Boomers and the Challenger explosion for Gen Xers. Along with other school shootings, Columbine conveyed the message that the world, even at school, is not a safe place. Many youth workers have expressed the view that events like Columbine are only the tip of the iceberg in understanding today's teenagers. Millennials get steady doses of violence from their music, music videos, video games, real life news reports out of Iraq and Afghanistan, the war on terrorism, and the streets of their neighborhoods and cities. Under the well-scrubbed veneer of suburban Millennials, a dark side resides that is poorly understood by older generations.

In his book *Hurt: Inside the World of Today's Teenagers*, Chap Clark records the comments of a teenager that helps alert us to a dangerous façade: "People think I have the 'perfect' life. I wear the right clothes, I hang with the 'cool crowd,' my family has money. But the funny thing is, they don't know that I cry myself to sleep every night because my dad's expectations are impossible. I struggle with keeping up with school work. I come from a divorced home. They never see the real me. I have to put on a mask. I deal with the struggles of beer and alcohol. They don't know."[1] The complex world of Millennials will offer a significant challenge to churches or anyone who desires to minister to this generation.

In commenting on the life experiences of the Millennial Generation, Neil Howe and William Strauss, authors of *Millennials Rising*, give us a more optimisitic picture of Millennials:

> For the post-X Millennial Generation, those born since 1982 who now fill grade schools and the first two years of college, 9/11 is a defining moment. At a personal level, 9/11 affected them the least, since their own world endured a similar, if smaller-scale, "terrorism" crisis back in 1998-99, with the wave of Columbine-style school shootings. Polls show that kids have been the least surprised by new security

measures since they're the most used to having ID cards examined, luggage searched, and jokes screened by authorities. Today's kids trust and confide in authorities, set up Web cams in their rooms, and keep in constant electronic contact with parents and friends. For better or worse, privacy isn't a big issue among teens, and challenges to civil liberties are less of a worry than to older people.

Even before 9/11, the budding character of these new youth was making itself clear, with high trust in authority; rising achievement in math and science; and falling rates of crime, teen pregnancy, and substance abuse. Energized by a sense of their collective potential, large numbers of Millennials had already begun participating in community service. It was almost as though America was preparing these kids for some great mission. But what?

Along came 9/11, which may be history's answer to this question.[2]

The rapid advances in technology have leveled the information playing field and given Millennials a sense of control over their own destiny. Most any kind of knowledge can now be accessed through our fingertips or voice, opening a world with many options. The Internet has become a major source of education in our culture, especially for the Millennial Generation. Wireless technology is not a novelty for this generation. Instead, it has become integrated into their school, work, and social lives, allowing them to be footloose while staying connected to friends, family, and the world. Millennials have become the "always-on generation," awash in a world of cell phones, notebook computers, MP3 players, camera phones, video games, digital photos and video clips, instant and text messaging, Facebook, YouTube, Twitter, music videos, DVD players, iPods, ATMs and more. Evidence is mounting that they will spend more time in the virtual world than the real world—often late into the night and early morning. It is not surprising that a National Sleep Foundation poll found that one-third of Millennials report that they are sleepy during the daytime. Some observers argue that constant use of technological gadgets has also given Millennials a short attention span.

Technology has helped drive the globalization process that has swept the world over the past several decades. Our globalized world is now a smaller village and a larger playground for Millennials. It is not uncommon for teenagers to regularly communicate online with their contemporaries all over the globe. Consequently, Millennials in the United States feel more at home in the world than do previous generations. Since the Cold War has been relegated to the scrap heap of history, new geopolitical alignments and increasing global chaos has changed the way this generation views the world. The globalization process has been further driven by immigration and the increasing diversity of America's and the world's populations. In the United States, the population of the Millennial Generation is one third nonwhite. The open attitudes of Millennials to diversity will lead to a more multiracial and multiethnic society in the future.

In addition to globalization, the urbanization of America and the rest of the world have helped shape the profile of the Millennial Generation. American youth culture has become urbanized, even for Millennials living in rural America. For example, the hip-hop, rap, and Latino subcultures are not limited to our inner-city neighborhoods. These subcultures have also profoundly influenced youth culture in the suburbs and rural areas as well. Additionally, city centers in many metropolitan areas have become the playgrounds of Millennials and GenXers, allowing urban and suburban lifestyles to blend.

Over the past several decades, the American family has changed profoundly, deeply affecting the lives of Millennials. The families of many Millennials look a lot different than the families of previous generations. While the U.S. divorce rate has stabilized, more than one-third of Millennials will experience their parents' divorce. But unlike many Gen Xers, Millennials generally have the perspective that they were wanted by their parents. Many in this generation were born to Boomer parents who waited to have children and dearly wanted these children. Indications of parental attitudes toward their Millennial children were seen in the early 1980s as cars sported triangular signs announcing "Baby on Board." No ordinary babies, these were *trophy kids* whose later achievements graduated to the car bumper proclaiming, "My Child is an Honor Student at such-and-such School." Millennials are the children of the soccer moms who take their kids to multiple activities each week, if not each day. The parents of Millennials often center their world on their children.

With the coming of the Millennial Generation, several new issues found their way into the American social debate. Child abuse and child safety became hot topics as parents sought to protect their children. Parents also injected themselves into the educational life and experiences of their children. Home schooling became a popular alternative for parents of Millennials, and many today continue to closely monitor their child's educational progress even through college. (Many colleges have set up special offices to deal with meddling parents.) Character, virtues, values, and bullying became hotly debated topics among educators, politicians, and parents. Books and programs on virtues and values have also influenced the educational experiences of Millennials. But without question, the greatest influence of the Millennial Generation has come from pop culture.

Millennial Popular Culture

The influence of popular culture on emerging generations has become more pervasive over the past several decades. With much money to be made (and lost), marketers have fine tuned the power of pop culture to sell certain clothes, popularize certain music, boost the careers of certain stars, sell tickets to certain movies, and promote many other lucrative ventures. While many values and attitudes held by Millennials have been shaped by pop culture, the saturation of advertising has actually made them skeptical and savvy consumers—but consumers they are. According to many marketing reports, Millennials aged eight to twenty-one spend more than $200 billion a year on an ever-changing array of pop culture attractions. They show less brand loyalty than past generations and will create fads that quickly come and go. What's 'in' today is gone tomorrow. Millennials are increasingly going online to educate themselves about consumer items and to purchase these items. While this fast-moving consumerism is partially driv-

Peter Menconi

en by technology, it is also fueled by the vast number of options available to Millennials.

The impact of pop culture for older Millennials began in the early 1980s with the introduction of Nickelodeon, the first cable network targeted directly to children. Unlike children's shows from the major networks, Nickelodeon offered children the opportunity to watch their favorite shows most anytime they wanted. Original cartoons called *Nicktoons* also became popular among Millennial youngsters. The FOX Network entered the children's TV market in 1990 with *FOX Kids*. Hit shows such as *Batman: The Animated Series* and the *Mighty Morphin Power Rangers* fueled the imaginations of this generation. In 1992, young Millennials were given more viewing options with the launching of the Cartoon Network. Children in the second half of the generation grew up with Barney, the ever-present purple dinosaur.

As Millennials grew into adolescents, new celebrities emerged from this generation. Britney Spears, Leanne Rimes, Mandy Moore, and boy bands such as *NSYNC and the Back Street Boys were popular musical acts. MTV influenced Millennials, as it did Gen X, as musical artists and groups came and went at dizzying speeds. Hollywood and TV executives understood the economic power of this generation and began producing movies and TV shows targeting Millennials. As Hollywood replaced the child devils of the Gen X era with the child angels of the Millennials, the Olsen Twins, Lindsay Lohan, Kirsten Dunst, Elijah Wood, and other Millennials became stars to their generation. New television offerings targeted this generation with shows such as *Dawson's Creek, Malcolm in the Middle, Buffy*

130

the Vampire Slayer, Sabrina, Teenage Witch, Smallville, and others. Reality TV became popular among both Gen Xers and Millennials. TV technology now allows young adults to watch programs whenever they want and without commercial—"on demand" is expected by Millennials.

Time magazine ran a cover story in the summer of 1999 entitled "Sport Crazed Kids." The accompanying story told of the great number of Millennials involved in organized sports: "Some estimates put the number of American youths participating in various organized sports at 40 million. According to the Sporting Goods Manufacturers Association, the number of kids playing basketball now tops 12 million. Not to mention the nearly 7 million playing soccer. Or the 5 million playing baseball. Hockey, originally played on frozen ponds, is now a year-round sport involving more than half a million kids from Maine down through the Sunbelt."[3] While growing up, millions of Millennials joined a sport-crazed culture as they watched Michael Jordan and Tiger Woods ascend to super stardom. Their own generation has already produced sports stars such as LeBron James, Carmelo Anthony, Michelle Wie, Sidney Crosby, Danica Patrick, and Serena Williams. Many others will follow.

Millennial Values and Worldviews

The values and worldviews of Millennials differ somewhat from those of Gen Xers. While there is some overlap, the following table will summarize some of the similarities and differences that exist between the two generations:

	Millennials	Gen Xers
Basic philosophy	Postmodern	Postmodern
Motivation	Optimistic and altruistic	Pessimistic/self-absorbed
Work ethic	Doers and achievers	Play before work
Use of technology	Very comfortable	Comfortable
View of authority	Accepts authority	Resists authority
Attitudes toward parents	Generally like parents	Generally hurt by parents
Educational experience	Higher SAT/ACT scores, Higher number in college	Lower SAT/ACT scores, Lower number in college
Political activity	Higher number vote, Politically involved, More conservative	Lower number vote, Politically apathetic, More liberal
Diversity	One-third non-white, Multiethnic/multiracial	Appreciates diversity, but less diverse than Millennials
Emotional makeup	Less emotional, More pragmatic	Emotionally-sensitive, Emotionally-guarded
Relationships	Group and team oriented	Independent, though desiring community
Spirituality	Spirituality important, Mildly interested in organized religion	Spirituality important, little interest in organized religion

In their book *Millennials Rising*, Neil Howe and William Strauss call the Millennials the "next great generation." "Yes, there's a revolution under way among today's kids—a *good news revolution*. This generation is going to rebel by behaving not worse, but *better*. Their life mission will not be to tear down old institutions that don't work, but to build up new ones that do. Look closely at youth indicators, and you'll see that Millennial attitudes and behaviors represent a sharp break from Generation X, and are running exactly counter to trends launched by the Boomers. Across the board, Millennial kids are challenging a long list of common assumptions about what 'postmodern' young people must become."[4] They further contrast the differences between

132

Millennials and Gen X by asking questions and answering their own questions as follows:

- *Are Millennials another "lost" generation?* No. The better word is "found."
- *Are they pessimists?* No. They're optimists.
- *Are they self-absorbed?* No. They're cooperative team players.
- *Are they distrustful?* No. They accept authority.
- *Are they rule breakers?* No. They're rule followers.
- *Are they neglected?* No. They're the most watched over generation in memory.
- *Are they stupid?* No. They're smarter than most people think.
- *Have they given up on progress?* No. Today's kids believe in the future and see themselves as its cutting edge.[5]

Perhaps it can be said that the new three Rs of the Millennial Generation are rules, respect, and responsibility.

Like Gen X, the Millennial Generation continues and expands the postmodern worldview. For example, Millennials have only known a world that is globalized and diverse. They readily accept contradictory observations and realities as equally true. That is, in a postmodern world, "truth" is relative; absolute truth does not exist. Consequently, you may embrace your understanding of life as good and true, while someone else's worldview is equally good and true though it contradicts yours. When it comes to lifestyles, Millennials are quite pragmatic—"If it works for you, go with it."

Peter Menconi

In part because of this pragmatism, the Millennials arrive at their own unique views on various issues. Americans between the ages 15 and 92 were interviewed for a 2002 nationwide Pew Charitable Trusts survey. The results found that many Millennials held views that were more conservative than their older counterparts:

- While 69 percent of young people ages 15 to 26 supported prayer in public schools, only 59 percent of older adults favored it.
- Barely 34 percent of older adults favored restrictions on abortion, while 44 percent of youths 15 to 22 backed such limitations.
- Forty percent of adults favored federal aid to religious charities, while 59 percent of college-age young people supported the concept, and 67 percent of teenagers favored it.
- Young people had a more favorable view of Christian fundamentalists than their seniors, 33 percent compared with 26 percent.[6]

On other issues, Millennials were more liberal than their older contemporaries:

- Young people felt sexual content and violence on TV were less serious problems than did their elders.
- The younger generation was more concerned about discrimination and the environment than were older generations.[7]

Many Millennials are being raised in the more protected and controlled environment of a post-9/11 world. Their

Boomer parents, who already have a competitive bent, are encouraging accelerated academics and cooperative behavior to insure that their children make it in an increasingly chaotic world. News articles with titles such as *The Crème de la Crème Preschool, Burdened by their Books* and *The Overwhelmed Child* chronicled the crafting of the Millennials into a generation of trophy kids. They have grown up with "Just Say No," MADD (Mothers Against Drunk Driving), SADD (Students Against Drunk Driving), community service projects, "See You at the Pole," character education, and many other adult-initiated programs. The following cartoon by R.J. Matson succinctly depicts the evolving differences between the Boomers, the Gen Xers, and the Millennials.

(Cartoon by R.J. Matson from <u>www.millennialsrising. com</u>. Used by permission.)

A national opinion survey of college freshman by Louis Harris and Associates, called *Generation 2001*, found that parents, family, religion, and generosity are central to America's next generation. The majority of students indicated that the people they most respected and admired were their moms and dads. (Certainly, Gen Xers would not have answered this way during their college-aged years.) The respondents to the survey also said that honesty and integrity were behaviors important to them. The *Generation 2001* survey of Millennials found that:

- 75 percent believe in life after death, and most say religion's a big part of life.
- 89 percent believe in God, and nearly 70 percent attend religious services.
- 90 percent agree that helping others is more important than helping oneself.
- 73 percent report having volunteered services to schools, charities, and church.
- 96 percent plan to marry at an average age of 26 years.
- 91 percent hope to have children, with an average of three children desired.[8]

Millennial Spirituality

While a great majority of Millennials indicated they believe in God, a closer look at their spirituality is necessary. Many Millennials define "God" significantly different than do GIs, Silents and most Boomers. The postmodern understanding of God and spirituality that began with the Boomers and was accelerated by Gen Xers has reached new levels with the Millennials. In fact, their view of God is not only postmodern but it is also post-Christian. That is, many Millennials embrace a pluralistic understanding of God and a spirituality that makes room for many valid expressions of faith and many roads to God. Even those Millennials who profess faith in Jesus Christ see themselves more as *followers of Jesus* and not necessarily *Christians*.

Millennial spirituality has been shaped by several major cultural and social influences. First, through their (usually) Boomer parents and their (usually) Boomer teachers, Millennials have been taught to thrive on change, to embrace and value diversity, and to be unwaveringly tolerant and politically correct. Consequently, God's unchanging truth is really not absolute truth but is relative to each person and their unique life situation. Second, the profound changes in sexual behavior and mores, coupled with the redefinition of the family, have led to significant moral confusion among Millennials. Again, relativism and pragmatism have led Millennials to practical amorality where each person decides what is right in his or her own eyes.

A clearer understanding of Millennial spirituality is provided for us by Christian Smith and Melinda Lundquist Denton in their book *Soul Searching: The Religious and Spiritual Lives of American Teenagers*. As researchers with the National Study of Youth and Religion, the authors interviewed thousands of teenagers and their parents and uncovered some surprising findings. First, the study found that unlike Gen Xers, there is relatively little spiritual seeking among Millennials. In fact, many of them readily and unquestioningly accept the religion in which they were raised. Second, Smith and Denton found that the beliefs of teenaged Millennials could be condensed and summarized into a religious viewpoint they call Moralistic Therapeutic Deism. The authors describe the basic tenets of Moralistic Therapeutic

Peter Menconi

Deism as follows: (1) A God exists who created and ordered the world and watches over human life on earth; (2) God wants people to be good, nice, and fair to each other, as taught in the Bible and by most world religions; (3) the central goal of life is to be happy and to feel good about oneself; (4) God does not need to be particularly involved in one's life except when he is needed to resolve a problem; and (5) good people go to heaven when they die.[9]

It would be easy for ministry leaders to misinterpret the spiritual understanding and desires of Millennials. On the outside they may appear to have their spiritual lives together while on the inside there is little foundational understanding about their faith. When Millennials desire to grow an authentic relationship with Jesus Christ, they have certain expectations on how it will proceed. They expect their worship experiences within and without the church to be authentic, real, and sincere. That is, they readily identify and reject religious activities and programs that do not genuinely bring them closer to God. In her book *Generation 2K: What Parents and Others Need to Know About the Millennials,* Wendy Murray Zoba writes, "Moral ambiguity has spurred [Millennials] to want decisive boundaries and real answers. Spiritual longing has made them ready to give it everything they've got in their quest for God."[10] It is clear that growing Millennials in their journey with Jesus presents ministry leaders with a challenging task. It is also clear that Millennials, and the Gen Xers who preceded them, need relationships with members of the older generations to provide a perspective and context for their spiritual searches.

Part 3
Toward An Intergenerational Church

Chapter 8
Intergenerational Tension

With a better understanding of the current generations in the church, let's now look at how to translate generational differences into intergenerational unity. It is safe to say that if a church is multigenerational, it has intergenerational tension. Pastors, church leaders, and attendees must first acknowledge that intergenerational tension may exist in their congregations. Tension can exist between any of the generations, but it is usually most prevalent between contiguous generations. In the song *The Living Years*, Mike and the Mechanics sing "Every generation blames the one before and all of their frustrations come beating on your door." It seems every generation has to blame someone for the stress and chaos that accompanies coming of age and usually it is the preceding generation that receives this blame.

In *Bridging Divided Worlds: Generational Cultures in Congregations*, Jackson W. Carroll and Wade Clark Roof write:

> A congregation may thus be thought of as an arena of conflict, as a setting in which contestation over moral and lifestyle issues as well as styles of reli-

gious belief and practice may erupt at any time. For this reason, the symbolic world uniting members of a congregation is precarious and rests upon a complex set of social processes. Unity within a congregation, and especially unity across the generations, depends upon local tradition, and perhaps most of all upon skillful manipulation on the part of religious leaders of the "ties that bind." Pastors know that there must be ongoing negotiations of those ties and work at unifying the social bonds within a congregation. Savvy pastors know they must deliberately try to build bridges of understanding across generational lines.[1]

In this chapter we will take a closer look at some potential areas of intergenerational tension and conflict that can exist in a local church.

Tension Between GIs and Silents

As members of the GI Generation leave us, the residual tension between GIs and Silents is greatly diminishing. Having lived in the shadow of the greatest generation, many Silents were irritated by the dominance of the GIs. As GIs founded and led our growing post-WWII corporations and institutions, including the church, Silents often were given the secondary roles of management. Members of the Silent Generation were typically not allowed to lead, but instead, were to follow in the wake of their GI leaders. As they pass on, however, GIs have relinquished the reins of leadership in many churches to Silents. Whenever they have leadership opportunities in churches or denominations, Silents have primarily functioned as managers and not visionary leaders. For example, denominational rules and bureaucracy have grown under Silent leadership. These leaders' fondness for order often annoys emerging Boomer leaders, creating tension between these generations.

Tension Between Silents and Boomers

Unfortunately, Silents often inherit the leadership reins from GIs in dying churches, meaning revitalization will be difficult. Even in healthy churches where Silents obtain leadership roles, Boomers often preempt these roles. They are generally more aggressive than Silents in pushing themselves to the front. Silents often resent upstart Boomers who think the world centers around them and their needs. Tension between these two generations primarily results when the needs and desires of Silents are unceremoniously pushed aside. While the Silent Generation still values many traditional activities and practices of the local church, many Boomers do not. For example, an obvious source of intergenerational tension results when a church moves from a Silent-preferred traditional worship service format to a Boomer-preferred contemporary or blended service. The cry of "We have always done it this way" can drive a hard and fast wedge between Silents, Boomers, and other generations in the church.

In *Bridging Divided Worlds*, Carroll and Roof surfaced this tension in their research:

> Sharply contrasting preferences in worship style and music have led to what some call "worship wars" in many congregations, with a younger generation asking for contemporary liturgy and music while an older generation finds the newer forms spiritu-

> ally unpalatable. The choice of liturgy and music is more than a preference, it is a symbolic expression of identity and of religious meaning implicit within that identity.

> Who has the authority to make decisions about these things? Usually authority rests with the official leadership, drawn predominately from the pre-boomer generation, while a growing number of new members are from the younger cohorts, boomers and Xers. Religious leaders often find themselves caught in the crossfire between opposing factions, with one wanting change, the other wanting to maintain the status quo; or clergy may not understand or appreciate the preference of a generation different from their own.[2]

Another common source of intergenerational tension between these two generations may result from their differing views of Christian education. In reality, Silents are the last generation to value Sunday school classes where the teacher merely lectures. Silents value expert teaching, information, and knowledge. In fact, many Silents equate spiritual growth with obtaining more information and knowledge, especially Bible knowledge. By contrast, Boomers need learning experiences that are interactive. They believe that their perspective is often as good and valuable as that of the teacher or leader. Silents will sit quietly and listen; Boomers often will not, preferring interaction.

The general demeanor of Boomers often offends Silents. From a young age Boomers have been the central focus of most activity. Consequently, they think they are and should be the center of most church activity. Silents often see this behavior as self-centered and indulgent; they are used to more discreet, well-mannered relationships. Despite this relational tension, rarely will Silents directly challenge Boomers; it is not their style. Instead, they may simply leave a congregation led by Boomers and move to a Silent-dominated church.

If a church wants to keep and successfully utilize the two generations in leadership, they will need to facilitate communication and understanding between Silents and Boomers. One way of improving relationships between the two generations is simply have them spend more time together, getting to know each other better. Another helpful approach is to have leaders of different generations talk about and focus on their common concerns and mission for their church. Members of each generation usually have different skills and experiences that can complement one another, making a church more effective in ministry.

Tension Between Boomers and Gen Xers

The primary tension between Boomers and Gen Xers is not usually over *style*, but over *substance*. That is, differences in music and worship styles create only superficial tensions between these two generations. The deeper divide and tension grows out of the overall feeling by Gen Xers that Boomers are self-centered and not to be trusted. In addition, many Xers believe Boomers have been poor parents who abandoned their family responsibilities, leaving many Gen Xers to raise themselves. In short, Gen Xers feel deeply wounded by the way they have been treated by Boomers in the home, workplace, church, and society at large. From the time they came of age, Gen Xers were unfairly labeled as slackers, and they have had a difficult time shaking off the tag. Many Xers blame Boomers for this label. Since Gen Xers value their personal lives at least as much as their work lives, they appear as slackers when compared with more work oriented Boomers.

Local churches have been directly affected by the tension between Boomers and Gen Xers. For example, Xers remain the most poorly represented generation in the church since many want little to do with organized religion, especially if Boomers organize it. In Gen Xers' postmodern world, a personal spiritual journey does not need a church. They do not want any part of an old-time religion that has been party to the hurt and pain many of them feel. A 2003 study by the Barna Research Group confirms that young Gen Xers are having a difficult time relating to the local church:

> Millions of twentysomething Americans—many of whom were active in churches during their teens— pass through their most formative adult decade while putting Christianity on the backburner. The research, conducted with 2,660 twentysomethings, shows that Americans in their twenties are significantly less likely than any other age group to attend church services, to donate to churches, to be absolutely committed to Christianity, to read the Bible, or to serve as a volunteer or lay leader in churches.[3]

One Gen X response to their discontent with existing churches is to create churches to their liking. For more than a decade, there has been a movement to create Generation

X-driven churches that meet the needs of their generation. This movement has been dubbed the "emerging/emergent church," the "postmodern church," the "alternative church," and the "church-within-a-church," among other names. Gen X churches usually incorporate music more acceptable to Xers; use drama and art as expressions of one's spiritual journey and search; design opportunities for interaction and community; use technology to draw closer to God; respond to the needs of society and the world in hands-on ways; reach back for pre-modern church connection; and integrate other less traditional forms of spiritual expressions. One major driving force in the Gen X-dominated church is to find and develop *community*. Gen Xers so badly want authentic and genuine community and relationships but are generally poorly equipped to develop them.

Another point of contention that can lead to intergenerational tension between these two generations is that many Gen Xers feel Boomers find anything and everything acceptable. Stated another way, Gen Xers believe that Boomers have poorly defined standards of right and wrong. Since many members of Generation X were raised with little parental guidance, they are looking for authentic direction that will add greater meaning to their lives. They generally do not believe that Boomers can provide this guidance for them. Gen Xers are more likely to seek direction and guidance from Silents or GIs. Consequently, multigenerational churches have an excellent opportunity to build bridges of communication between Gen Xers and these older generations.

The themes of the worship songs created by Gen Xers usually address God as the only one who can heal the wounds of their souls and fill their deepest needs. Again, Gen Xers have no need for the congregation—each individual, with God, can make it work. With this motivation, Gen X song writers and musicians have written some wonderful worship music. It's ironic that Boomers have readily incorporated much Gen X music into their worship services and style. Boomers have no problem taking what they want and need from multiple sources. This Boomer knack of making their generation the center of activity has created intergenerational tension with both Silents and Xers.

Tension Between Gen Xers and Millennials

The intergenerational tension between these two groups is just beginning to surface. Gen Xers are now recognizing the significant differences between themselves and Millennials. Generally speaking, Millennials are less concerned about the internal processes of emotional and spiritual healing than Gen Xers and more concerned about pragmatic and useful results. Millennials will often attend Gen X churches and worship services as one of several spiritual experiences and options as they look for the best fit that meets their needs. There is growing evidence that Millennials are more ambitious and focused than are their older Gen X counterparts, creating the real possibility that they will grow impatient and weary of the self-conscious angst of Gen Xers.

Millennials have had less tension with Boomers than have Gen Xers. Instead of following the lead of Gen Xers, Millennials may regularly attend Boomer-driven churches. In the near future, there is a real danger that Gen Xers will find themselves sandwiched between two powerful generations, resulting in Xers seeing the local church as an even more unfriendly place. As an alternative, Gen Xers will continue to look elsewhere for their spiritual needs to be met. House churches, small groups, blogs, and other forms of interaction may increasingly meet the spiritual needs of Xers. Unfortunately, these responses may only serve to further isolate Gen Xers from the generations that precede and follow them. In reality, the intergenerational tension between Gen Xers and Millennials is yet to be fully understood and played out.

Multigenerational Tension

Intergenerational tension not only exists between contiguous generations, but also between any generations in society and the church. For example, members of the GI and Silent Generations both have difficulty accepting the rock music of the younger generations. Conversely, Gen Xers and Millennials do not usually relate to the traditional worship service favored by GIs and Silents, and simply will not attend. As the swing generation, Boomer-dominated churches offer the greatest potential for either significant unity or considerable discord since Boomer churches are the ones most likely attended by all generations. Boomers can either be the transitional group that bridges the generational gaps or lightning rods of discontent for all the other generations.

Increasingly, churches are choosing not to address intergenerational tensions. Instead, they are providing separate venues for each generation to have their needs met. Especially in large churches, leaders are coping with intergenerational tension by providing multiple worship services of various styles. For GIs and Silents, a traditional service is provided, often with organ music, robed choir, beloved hymns, and set liturgy. The same church might also have a contemporary service with a praise band of guitars, drums, and keyboards in a more informal atmosphere with contemporary choruses and group participation. Further, they may opt for a blended service that incorporates both traditional and contemporary elements of worship. The same church may even have an emergent, Generation X, or postmodern service with a worship team, regular use of drama and the arts, various multimedia productions, candles, and an eclectic blend of the old and the new.

While attempting to cater to all generations, these "church-within-a-church" approaches to managing intergenerational tensions in reality succeed in isolating generations, not uniting them. Not only will age-based ministries lead to greater splintering in the congregation, but they can also be counterproductive for families and households, further dividing an already fragmented society. Scripture calls us to unity within the face of diversity, whether that diversity is in age, race, socioeconomic position, gender, or any other measure. Christian unity in the face of diversity is a clear imperative, according to the apostle Paul: *"Just as each of us has one body with many members, and these members do not all have the same function, so in Christ we who are many form one body, and each member belongs to all the others."—Romans 12:4-5.*

Intergenerational Apathy

Perhaps the most destructive consequence of intergenerational tension is apathy. When people of different generations stop caring about each other, we are all in serious peril. One of the most obvious manifestations of this apathy surfaces as ageism, the attitudes and acts of prejudice and discrimination directed against other people based on their chronological age. Ageism takes numerous forms. In their book *The New Senior,* Charles and Win Arn write "Our society finds little use for the elderly. It defines them as useless, forces them to retire before they have exhausted their capacity for work, and reinforces their sense of superfluity at every opportunity."[4] Quite to the contrary, recent research among the elderly has shown that chronological age is not a good predictor of much of anything. In his book *The Virtues of Aging*, President Jimmy Carter writes, "So then, when *are* we old? The correct answer is that each of us is old when we *think* we are—when we accept an attitude of dormancy, dependence on others, a substantial limitation on our physical and mental activity, and restrictions on the number of other people with whom we interact."[5]

Despite America's continuing obsession with youth, ageism also can be aimed at young people. While it has been somewhat traditional to see teenagers as undependable and random, adolescence now often extends to twentysomethings. Gen Xers especially have reinforced the stereotype that young adults take longer to grow up and launch. Employers will often not hire young adults who have no experience, the same young adults who cannot get experience without being hired. Yet, many young people are quite responsible and have helpful opinions on a wide variety of subjects and issues. Older adults would be wise to engage teenagers and young adults in meaningful conversations, and young people can benefit greatly from the experience and perspective of the older generations. All age groups will find that the others have much to offer.

Chapter 9
Intergenerational Mission

While intergenerational tension is a reality in most churches, it can be minimized. The most effective way to turn this tension into an asset is to involve all generations in defining the primary mission of the church. Although many differing views will be offered, all generations should focus on the mission of the church succinctly given by Jesus in the greatest commandment and Great Commission:

> *"'Love the Lord your God with all your heart and with all your soul and with all your mind.' This is the first and greatest commandment. And the second is like it: 'Love your neighbor as yourself.' All the Law and the Prophets hang on these two commandments."*
> *- Matthew 22:37-40*

> *"All authority in heaven and on earth has been given to me. Therefore go and make disciples of all nations, baptizing them in the name of the Father and of the Son and of the Holy Spirit, and teaching them to obey everything I have commanded you."*
> *- Matthew 28:18-20*

Before church leaders of all generations come to a consensus on the mission of the church, they must hear and discuss the many viewpoints offered. Newer terms are now being bantered about when describing the local church: the "emerging church," the "missional church," the "attractional church," the "incarnational church," the "deep church" and many other vaguely descriptive terms. As American churches wrestle with the challenges of communicating the Gospel to a changing society, new ideas need to be discussed and tried. All of this discussion and experimentation only underscores the transitions that lie ahead for local churches. While the discussion of these ministry concepts may be new to older church leaders, they must listen, learn, and contribute. They will need to work hard to survive and thrive in the mine field of ministry that lies ahead.

As church leaders of different generations discuss the mission of their church, it is helpful to define the terms being used. Most churches in America have their roots in the *attractional* model where a local church teaches and preaches a theology, practices a worship style, and establishes ministry programs. In addition, the attractional church may identify with a specific denomination or religious tradition. All ministry activities give the church a specific identity with the expectation that people, attracted to its uniqueness, will attend. Most of the attractional church's ministries take place within the walls of their building, as they practice the *Field of Dreams* adage: "If you build it, *they* will come." The attractional church is illustrated in the following diagram:

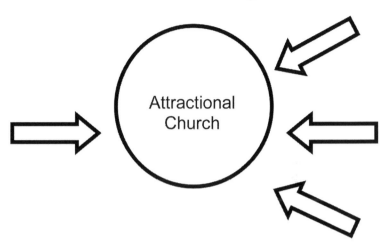

With this model, the attractional church offers a variety of programs that attendees come to "consume." Building on the historical model of a traditional church, the attractional church is a one-stop gathering place for people to have their spiritual needs met from birth to marriage to death. Most attractional church attendees are fairly homogeneous, usually look and act alike, are socio-economically similar, and generally live comparable lifestyles. This sameness makes attractional churches less appealing to younger generations who are more at home in a diverse world.

Increasingly, fewer and fewer people are attracted to attractional churches. This is especially true of young adults. As noted previously, many young adults consider themselves spiritual, but most do not want to commit to or even associate with a local church. Consequently, many young pastors and leaders are calling for a radical change in the way we "do" church, leading to a fresh conversation about the church experience over the past couple of decades. While this conversation or movement goes by a variety of names such as the emerging church, the post-modern church, the post-Christian church, the missional church, and other labels, its primary motivation is to become the *incarnational* church. An incarnational approach to ministry draws on the life of Jesus Christ and the early church's example of taking the gospel outside the walls of the religious subculture and into an unbelieving society. In short, incarnational means "in the flesh," and advocates of an incarnational church believe the gospel should be lived out by Jesus' followers on a 24/7 basis. In his book *LeadershipNext: Changing Leaders in a Changing Culture*, Eddie Gibbs gives us insight into the incarnational approach to ministry:

> The church is challenged to take up an incarnational approach. Using the example of Jesus' ministry and the struggle of the New Testament church to relate the gospel to both non-Jews and Jews, the church today must not extract inquirers and seekers from their cultural context only to invite them into a secure cocoon. Instead, it must permeate the cultural context in order to learn its values and aspirations in order to relate the gospel effectively. In so doing, those who are engaged in mission will come to a fresh understanding of the gospel and will face the gospel's challenges afresh in their own lives.[1]

As they move out into the culture, incarnational churches can be found in coffeehouses, art galleries, homes, online, and many other novel venues.

The differences between attractional church advocates and incarnational church supporters may look like this:

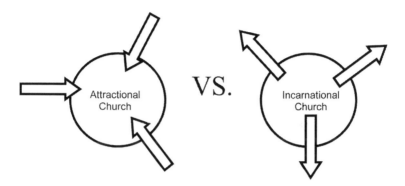

As pastors and church leaders move toward defining and implementing the mission of their church, the discussion should *not* be about the attractional or traditional church versus the incarnational or emerging church. The mission of either and all types of churches should be the same, just implemented differently. If Jesus' greatest commandment and Great Commission are accepted as the basic template for a church's mission, then the local church must be both attractional *and* incarnational. In fact, the church that is truly both attractional and incarnational is more fully *missional*.

Because the term "missional" is being bantered about in so many different contexts, it needs to be more clearly defined. In their book *Missional Church: A Vision for the Sending of the Church in North America*, Darrell L. Guder and other contributors offered several defining characteristics of the missional church:

With the term *missional* we emphasize the essential nature and vocation of the church as God's called and sent people:

1. A missional ecclesiology is biblical. Whatever one believes about the church needs to be found in and based on what the Bible teaches.
2. A missional ecclesiology is historical. Today this means reading our Western history and the worldview emergence of the church carefully.
3. A missional ecclesiology is contextual. There is but one way to be the church, and that is incarnationally, within a specific concrete setting.
4. A missional ecclesiology is eschatological. New biblical insights will convert the church and its theology; new historical challenges will raise questions never before considered; and new cultural contexts will require a witnessing response that redefines how we function and how we hope as Christians.
5. A missional ecclesiology can be practiced, that is, it can be translated into practice. The basic function of all theology is to equip the church for its calling.[2]

In his book *The Emerging Church*, Dan Kimball gives a more succinct definition, describing the missional church as "A body of people sent on a mission who gather in community for worship, encouragement, and teaching from the Word that supplements what they are feeding themselves throughout the week."[3] But perhaps the best way to understand the missional church is to identify the shift that is taking place in the way emerging groups are understanding the mission of the church. In their book *Breaking the Missional Code: Your Church Can Become a Missionary in Your Community*, Ed Stetzer and David Putnam list the shifts that are taking place from the traditional church to the missional church:

- from programs to processes,
- from demographics to discernment,
- from models to missions,
- from attractional to incarnational,
- from uniformity to diversity,
- from professional to passionate,
- from seating to sending,
- from decisions to disciples,
- from additional to exponential, and
- from monuments to movements.[4]

In light of these current shifts, a local church should endeavor to be as attractional *and* incarnational as possible. In reality, the most exciting ministries of the church will be where these two areas overlap:

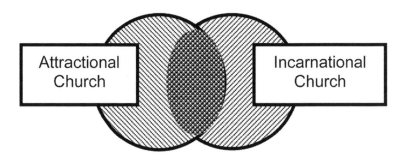

Peter Menconi

The goal in a truly missional church is to see as many people as possible in the congregation be participants in both attractional and incarnational ministries. In short, our call as followers of Jesus Christ is for seven days a week, and not just limited to Saturday nights or Sunday mornings.

As church leaders enter the discussion on the American church in transition, many good books, articles, and online resources can help. Most of these resources are long on diagnosing the problems and shortcomings of today's churches, but short on specific recommendations for change. In reality, churches and their leadership can be offered guidance toward change, but each church must *work out their own salvation*. There is no one-size-fits-all manual for change toward missional ministry. This is especially true when leading change from a multigenerational congregation to an intergenerational church.

Nevertheless, help is available. One of the better resources that will guide discussion among leaders of different generations is a book by Reggie McNeal titled *The Present Future: Six Tough Questions for the Church*. McNeal presents six new realities of church ministry and offers readers the wrong questions to avoid and the tough questions to ask. A summary of his major concepts provides discussion points for church leaders:

- New Reality 1: The collapse of the church culture.
  a) Wrong question: How do we do church better?
  b) Tough question: How do we convert from "churchianity" to Christianity?
- New Reality 2: The shift from church growth to kingdom growth.

- a) Wrong question: How do we grow this church?
- b) Tough question: How do we transform our community?
- New Reality 3: A new reformation: Releasing God's people
  - a) Wrong question: How do we turn members into ministers?
  - b) Tough question: How do we turn members into missionaries?
- New Reality 4: The return to spiritual formation.
  - a) Wrong question: How do we develop church members?
  - b) Tough question: How do we develop followers of Jesus?
- New Reality 5: The shift from planning to preparation.
  - a) Wrong question: How do we plan for the future?
  - b) Tough question: How do we prepare for the future?
- New Reality 6: The rise of apostolic leadership.
  - a) Wrong question: How do we develop leaders for church work?
  - b) Tough question: How do we develop leaders for the Christian movement?[5]

In his mildly controversial book *Revolution: Finding Vibrant Faith Beyond the Walls of the Sanctuary*, George Barna believes that the church in America is going through a revolutionary transition. He points to seven indicating trends:

- **Trend 1: The Changing of the Guard.** Younger leaders are moving into church leadership.

- **Trend 2: The Rise of a New View of Life.** A postmodern worldview is becoming more prevalent.

- **Trend 3: Dismissing the Irrelevant.** Activities that are not useful and impactful are readily abandoned.

- **Trend 4: The Impact of Technology.** Advances in technology are changing the context of contemporary ministry.

- **Trends 5: Genuine Relationships.** Younger generations are looking for relationships that are real, authentic, and inclusive.

- **Trends 6: Participation in Reality.** Enthusiasm is growing for a hands-on faith that takes believers into the world.

- **Trends 7: Finding True Meaning.** Believers are revisiting the importance of sacrifice and suffering in following Jesus Christ.[6]

Whatever tools are used to stimulate interaction between the generations isn't as important as beginning *and* continuing the discussion. Church leadership that wants to cultivate an intergenerational congregation will need to lead in a chaotic and shifting environment, but lead they must. As difficult as it may be to acknowledge, most churches in America are at risk of becoming marginalized in society. Without change, they will become less significant and fade into irrelevance. To reverse this slide, churches must stop asking people to merely come *and* see. Instead, we must recover the church's original calling to "go and make disciples." As leaders meet to determine what this calling looks like for their church, all generations must be included in the discussion. When everyone in the church is growing in their journey with Jesus, the mission of the church is realized.

Chapter 10
Intergenerational Leadership

In the past several decades, there are few subjects that have been more written and spoken about than *leadership*. Perhaps because we believe there are so few good leaders or because we do not understand true leadership, we seem to spend an excessive amount of time and energy on it. In most local churches and national denominations, effective intergenerational leadership is rare. Leaders from one generation usually provide a strong generational flavor for the local church, leaving little room for new ideas. Even in more progressive churches there is often one predominate generation that is slow to adopt changes that would benefit the spiritual lives of other generations. If local churches are to grow and flourish, good intergenerational leadership is imperative. While pressure for such leadership is building, most local churches do not have enough age diversity to fill this need. For this reason we will continue to see stagnation and slow death of many churches.

Though ideal and necessary, good intergenerational leadership is not easy to establish and maintain. While the Boomer-led church has the best chance of making the transition to intergenerational leadership, all churches can make this change. When establishing such leadership within a local church, several realities must be considered:

- Foremost, there must be an appreciation of all the generations in the church. A basic attitude recognizing that all the generations have something to offer is critical, and stereotyping between generations must be minimized.
- Incumbent leaders must be willing to share leadership power with members of other generations.
- Older leaders should not "pull rank" on younger leaders with father (or mother)-knows-best thinking. That is, more years on Earth does not necessarily mean more wisdom or insight. There are plenty of old fools leading some of our churches.
- Most leaders see the world from a generational perspective; their life experiences have shaped the way they see reality. Because they have learned certain ways that things work, it is difficult for them to imagine that there actually may be other effective ways of doing things. There are.
- Effective intergenerational leaders will not be afraid to change. While older leaders may want business as usual, they must realize that change is necessary in our rapidly shifting world. To complicate matters further, many younger leaders believe that anything that is new is right and good, while believing that anything that is old or traditional is wrong. Younger leaders must recognize that the axiom that "if we ignore history, we will repeat

the mistakes of the past" is still true. A church with good intergenerational leadership will have an understanding of the past and the good that can be taken from it, while having eyes on the exciting future.

• There is a tendency of leaders of all the generations to make *style* more important than *substance*. Leaders of all generations must ask themselves, and each other, "What is the purpose of the Church and of our local church?" The church exists to glorify God and not to meet our individual needs. Yet, many intergenerational battles have been fought over the need for leaders and church members of each age group to have their unique needs met. Intergenerational leaders must avoid the trap of majoring in minors and instead, focus on the primary call of the church.

• Intergenerational leaders should develop their spiritual lives together. They can and will learn from each other if they spend a significant amount of time together, not only praying and planning, but also having fun together.

• Intergenerational leaders should together review the biblical characteristics of a good leader. The example of Jesus Christ, who modeled the servant leader described in Philippians 2, is a good place to start:

Each of you should look not only to your own interests, but also to the interests of others. Your attitude should be the same as that of Christ Jesus: Who, being in very nature God, did not consider equality with God something

> to be grasped, but made himself nothing, taking the very nature of a servant, being made in human likeness. And being found in appearance as a man, he humbled himself and became obedient to death—even death on a cross!

Another good study for intergenerational leaders is to discuss the fruit of the Spirit and their relevance in each life and the life of the church. Galatians 5:22 and 23 enumerates these "fruits": love, joy, peace, patience, kindness, goodness, faithfulness, gentleness, and self-control, marks of spiritual maturity that provide important guidance for intergenerational leaders.

In addition, intergenerational leaders should read and discuss selected books on leadership. For example, they may want to discuss a book such as Andy Stanley's *The Next Generation Leader: Five Essentials for Those Who Will Shape the Future*. Stanley begins his book with a series of questions that are helpful for intergenerational leaders to discuss:

1. What are the leadership principles I wish someone had shared with me when I was a young leader?
2. What do I know now that I wish I had known then?
3. Of all that *could* be said about leadership, what must be conveyed to next generation leaders?[1]

He goes on to highlight five leadership concepts in the book that are excellent for an intergenerational discussion among leaders:

1.   *Competence:* Leaders must channel their energies toward those areas of leadership in which they are most likely to excel.

2.   *Courage:* The leader of an enterprise isn't always the smartest or most creative person on the team. He isn't necessarily the first to identify an opportunity. The leader is the one who has the courage to initiate, to set things in motion, to move ahead.

3.   *Clarity:* Uncertain times require clear directives from those in leadership. Yet the temptation for young leaders is to allow uncertainty to leave them paralyzed. A next generation leader must learn to be clear even when he is not certain.

4.   *Coaching:* You may be good. You may even be better than everyone else. But without a coach you will never be as good as you could be.

5.   *Character:* You can lead without character, but you won't be a leader worth following. Character provides next generation leaders with the moral authority necessary to bring together the people and resources needed to further an enterprise.[2]

Another book that addresses intergenerational leadership is *Leadership Divided: What Emerging Leaders Need and What You Might be Missing,* by Ron A. Carucci. In the book, Carucci's comparison of incumbent and emerging leaders is summarized below:

	Incumbent Leaders	Emerging Leaders
Rank	Have overly relied on hierarchy to make decisions; many still struggle with their use of authority.	Avoid the use of rank as a means of decision making and influence; seek to build consensus; for many, having power is terrifying; discomfort with authority without the approval of others.
Meaningful Conversation	Less comfortable with emotionally laden language and anything that feels "personal;" meaning is defined by results and clarity, not by connection.	Very comfortable expressing emotion and dealing with the emotions of others; become suspicious of those who seem emotionally guarded and won't self-disclose.
Inclusion/ Engagement	Have learned through dozens of team-building sessions the importance of including others in decisions that affect them; risk of being perceived as manipulative when stuck between wanting to do things their way but still wanting others to buy in.	Want everyone to enjoy the party equally; have limitless patience for lengthy decisions that allow all voices to be heard; invite others just for the sake of inclusion; risk paralysis and momentum loss owing to extensive involvement by many.
Dreaming	Believe that performance is about setting goals, monitoring progress, and measuring; think it's fine to allow others to have a vision as long as they keep commitments.	Could dream for days, and see most processes as unnecessarily bureaucratic and inhibiting creativity; very idealistic; they have a passion for a cause and want to achieve greatness; may struggle with holding others accountable for unmet commitments.
Generosity	Place a premium on developing those they most believe will in turn contribute to the organization; can be a bit blunt and awkward when giving developmental feedback; not comfortable disclosing personal shortcomings or failures.	Want to treat others with more equality and give liberally and evenly of their time and experience to others; are hungry to learn from the experiences and insights of incumbent leaders but without the expectation that they must "do it like I do;" want someone to guide them but can be willful when it comes to doing it their way.
Gratitude	Want to enthusiastically reward a job well done; appreciation is more commonly offered in exchange for outcomes; sincere compliments are offered as expressions of gratitude.	Want a champion who will cheer them on and care deeply for their talents and their results; they want to be appreciated for who they are as much as for what they can do; they need a lot of encouragement to stay in the game.

Source: *Leadership Divided: What Emerging Leaders Need and What You Might be Missing,* Ron A. Carucci, (San Francisco, CA: Jossey-Bass, 2006), 20- 21.

The transition of including emergent leaders into existing churches will be a major challenge. In his book *The Church in Transition*: *The Journey of Existing Churches into Emerging Churches*, Tim Conder gives us some of the reasons: "Those in the emergent culture tend to be weary of pastoral leadership that is overly individualized (all roads lead to a single vision), overly professionalized (the province of the ordained), overly technical (a specialized task and function orientation), and spiritually inaccessible (the spiritual life of a pastor being unique from any other person)."[3] It is quite apparent that a church that fails to raise up younger leaders will stagnate and die.

Older leaders have a responsibility to themselves and their congregations to develop and nurture new generations of leaders. The notion of leaving a legacy is not well developed in American culture. Yet throughout Scripture, a generational legacy among God's people was very important. Incumbent leaders must create opportunities to pass on and convey the wisdom they have learned through the experiences of their lives. Younger leaders can benefit from the insights of older leaders and avoid having to learn everything through trial and error. How ever the interchange takes place between the generations, it is clear that all will benefit from the sharing of different generational perspectives and viewpoints.

Another leadership challenge in the intergenerational church will be to develop missional leaders. These leaders have characteristics that differ from traditional leaders.

Peter Menconi

In their book *The Missional Leader: Equipping Your Church to Reach a Changing World,* Alan Roxburgh and Fred Romanuk give some insight into the character of a missional leader. They offer four personal qualities that are necessary for the missional leader: maturity, conflict management, personal courage, and trustworthiness and trusting. The following is a summary of their discussion on the character of a missional leader:

- Personal Maturity
  - Being authentic: The authentic leader is one whose actions and words are coherent and internally consistent.
  - Being self-aware: The self-aware leader takes the inner time to understand and find language for the God-shaped narrative of their lives.
- Conflict Management
  - Conflict is normal in change: Missional leaders can model ways of engaging conflict to bring about change.
  - No conflict, no movement: Missional leaders realize that the energy from conflict can grow us and make our relationships with others stronger.
  - Practice makes a difference: Leaders can learn the stages, steps, process, and inner workings of conflict resolution, but need the actual experience of entering into the process to improve their skills.

- Personal Courage
  - Missional leaders need personal courage to sacrifice popularity in order to tackle tough issues.
  - Personal courage can be learned and developed, but it can be realized only in the trenches of life, not in a classroom.
- Trustworthiness and Trusting
  - Without trust, missional transformation can never occur because it is the glue that enables a community to move forward in difficult times.
  - Trust operates as a barometer of interpersonal effectiveness.[4]

The role of leadership in the intergenerational church is critical. If leaders do not have a commitment to and an appreciation of all the generations in the church, the transition to an intergenerational church will fail. Churches may find that they will need to move certain leaders out of their roles in order to move forward. Guidelines for making this transition can be found in the teachings of Jesus and in other places in scripture. The "one another" passages are a good place to start. We are to love, honor, serve, forgive, comfort, exhort, and edify one another. The ancient guidelines for living righteously apply today as much as ever. Church leaders must take them seriously.

Chapter 11
Intergenerational Worship

Over the past several decades, the place of worship in many American churches has grown in importance. In his book *Planning Blended Worship,* Robert Webber states:

> Currently there is a growing awareness that worship is the central ministry of the Church. Worship is the center of the hourglass, the key to forming the inner life of the Church. Everything the Church does moves toward public worship, and all its ministries proceed from worship. Good worship creates community, evangelical warmth, hospitality to outsiders, inclusion of cultural diversity, leadership roles for men and women, intergenerational involvement, personal and community formation, healing, reconciliation, and other aspects of pastoral care. Because worship is itself an act of witness, it is the door to church growth, to missions and evangelism, and to issues of social justice. Worship now stands at the center of the Church's life and mission in the world.[3]

As noted earlier, worship and worship styles can be matters of great contention between generations in the local church. The development of a truly intergenerational worship style within the church is a difficult, but necessary task. The biggest barrier to achieving effective intergenerational worship is that *every* generation will want their style to dominate. The GIs and Silents will want the worship to be primarily traditional. The Boomers will want a contemporary worship experience to prevail. Gen Xers may not come if the worship time does not meet most of their postmodern criteria. (We have yet to see what Millennials will insist upon.) When confronted with generational resistance, it is tempting for pastors and church leaders to give everyone what they want. Effective intergenerational worship is not "throwing a bone" to each generation by simply offering a hymn for the GIs and Silents or a contemporary chorus for the Boomers or emergent music for the Gen Xers and Millennials. When running into resistance, it is also tempting to create multiple services to offer traditional worship, contemporary worship, postmodern worship, or any other worship style. As noted previously, a church-within-a-church approach creates a multigenerational church, not an intergenerational church.

The lively discussion over worship has helped raise it to a level of greater importance. It is incumbent on every follower of Jesus Christ to understand worship as best he or she can. In *Exploring the Worship Spectrum,* Paul Basden gives us some guidance by offering these major questions regarding worship:

- Should adoration of the one true God express itself in one true way of worship?

176

- Since God is one and longs for his people to be one, should our public worship be more unified than diverse?
- Does the freedom of worshipers compromise the integrity of the one we worship?
- Does worship preference reflect our legitimate freedom in Christ or our selfish sinful nature?
- Simply put, does God want all people to offer public worship to him in more or less the same way? Or does God affirm and bless all of our approaches that seek to give him glory and honor? And if he blesses some and not others, what are his criteria for rejecting those approaches that do not make the grade? [2]

In reality, worship is elusive, not well understood, and in need of greater clarification for all the generations. Again, in *Exploring the Worship Spectrum*, Paul Basden writes: Worship is inherently theological. It is primarily about God. Specifically, it is about how Christ-followers offer to God their love, gratitude, and praise. Several theologians have served us well by defining public worship in ways we can understand. For example:

- True worship is that exercise of human spirit that confronts us with the mystery and marvel of God in whose presence the appropriate and salutary response is adoring love.
- Christian worship is the glad response of Christians to the holy, redemptive love of God made known in Jesus Christ.

- Worship, in all its grades and kinds, is the response of the creature to the Eternal.
- The [Trinitarian] view of worship is that it is the gift of participating through the Spirit in the incarnate Son's communion with the Father.
- Worship…
  - quickens the conscience by the holiness of God,
  - feeds the mind with the truth of God,
  - purges the imagination by the beauty of God,
  - opens the heart to the love of God,
  - devotes the will to the purpose of God.[3]

Effective intergenerational worship is taking the best offerings each generation makes to God and blending them in a truly meaningful way. If the whole worship service is seen as the congregation's corporate offering to God, each generation within the church should have something meaningful to offer. Ideally, each element of the service should be integrated into a powerful statement about how we see and live our relationship with the God we worship. For example, a favorite GI or Silent Generation hymn may best express the theme or purpose of the worship service. Additionally, a dramatic reading, artistic performance, a movie clip, or a multimedia presentation may further enhance the worship experience. The point is that different people and generations worship God and grow in their faith in different ways. There is no *best* worship style. We can learn why this is true from each other and broaden our own ability to worship God. For example, God's attribute of love may be understood differently by different generations. By engaging in the worship experiences of all the generations, the whole congregation can grasp a more complete understanding of God and his love. A generational mosaic of worship can deepen and enrich our understanding of God.

While any style can work within an intergenerational church, blended worship has the greatest potential of bringing about unified worship among the generations. Effective blended worship actually takes all types of worship styles into account and draws from the best practices of each. Dr. Robert Webber has written extensively on blended worship:

> Worshiping churches freely borrow from other worship traditions. As a result, the four main traditions of worship today—liturgical, traditional Protestant, creative, and praise and worship—are undergoing a convergence of style.[4]

> The worship experience of many Christians is no longer isolated to a single tradition. Instead, a kind of cross-fertilization is occurring, and each tradition is borrowing from other traditions. I am convinced that borrowing, done intelligently and with spiritual sensitivity and then wisely integrated into worship, can have a powerful effect on a congregation's life.[5]

In the intergenerational church, this borrowing in worship is across generations as well as across traditions. However, cross-generational borrowing may be more difficult and less accepted than cross-traditional borrowing. For church leadership, cross-generational borrowing will

Peter Menconi

take work—and prayer. The establishment of effective intergenerational worship in a local church must be deliber-
ate and thoughtful. The following are some suggestions
on how congregations can move toward intergenerational
worship:

- There must be an appreciation of all the generations in the church. A basic attitude must
exist that recognizes that all the generations
have something to offer God and the church.
In fact, each generation will bring a unique
perspective on worshipping God that en-
riches the experiences of all the other generations.
- The worship leader and others should study
what the Bible has to say about worship. For
example, the worship of Abraham before God
was quite individual and personal. In Genesis
12:8 we read, "From there he (Abraham) went
on toward the hills east of Bethel and pitched
his tent, with Bethel on the west and Ai on
the east. There he built an altar to the LORD
and called on the name of the LORD." While
worship for the Israelites became more structured, it still had room for spontaneity. King
David was a passionate worshipper of God.
The Psalms give us some of the most impas-
sioned directives to worship:

    Ascribe to the LORD the glory due his
    name; worship the LORD in the splendor
    of his holiness. (Psalms 29:2)
    Come, let us bow down in worship, let
    us kneel before the LORD our Maker.
    (Psalms 95:6)

> Worship the LORD in the splendor of his holiness; tremble before him, all the earth. (Psalms 96:9)
> Worship the LORD with gladness; come before him with joyful songs. (Psalms 100:2)

Much more is said about worship in Scripture. Jesus' words to the Samaritan woman are words for us also to ponder. "God is spirit, and his worshipers must worship in spirit and in truth." (John 4:24)

- Involve multiple generations in worship as often as possible. Be sure that all generations are represented on a regular basis. Think creatively about how various generations can contribute to the worship time.
- Be sensitive to a variety of worship styles and incorporate these styles into worship. The use of various worship styles will teach each generation to appreciate other generations. We can all learn from each other.
- Use young and older singles and families of all compositions in worship.
- Have individuals from all generations share their stories and talk about their spiritual journeys with Jesus.
- Discover, cultivate, and use the musical and artistic gifts and talents of all generations.
- Thoughtfully assess your congregation and develop some worship experiences that are unique to your community.

Peter Menconi

Effective intergenerational worship will appreciate and utilize the contributions made by all styles of worship offered genuinely to God: the awe and mystery offered by liturgical worship; the theology and sincerity of hymn-based worship; the praise and passion of contemporary worship; the spirituality and enthusiasm of charismatic worship; the artistry and honesty of emergent worship.

Chapter 12
Intergenerational Preaching

We are beginning to hear and read comments that question the value and effectiveness of preaching in today's church and society. Some leaders in the emerging church have wondered aloud whether other ways of communicating God's truth may be more effective to a postmodern audience. Doug Pagitt, pastor of Solomon's Porch in Minneapolis wrote in a *FaithWorks* online article, "A sermon is often a violent act. It's a violence toward the will of people who have to sit there and take it."[1] In the same article, similar thoughts were expressed by Rudy Carrasco, associate director of the inner-city Harambee Center in Pasadena, Calif. Carrasco believes that preaching is often "too packaged and clean. Every day, every week, there's stuff that pops up in life, and it's not resolved, just crazy and confusing and painful. When people come across with three answers, and they know everything, and they have this iron sheen about them, I'm turned off. Period. I'm just turned off. And I think that's not unique to me."[2]

While the debate over the future and effectiveness of preaching will only heat up, the reality is that most pastors will continue to preach. So the question becomes, "How can we preach more effectively in the midst of rapid social change?" In an online article entitled "Getting Started in Postmodern Preaching," Dr. Dave Teague writes, "Postmodern preaching is more than communicating to a new generation. It is speaking to a new era."[3] He goes on to express what he believes are the most important elements of postmodern preaching:

- *Preach with Relevance:* It must connect with people.
- *Relevant Preaching Listens*: Postmoderns want to be listened to, not preached at. They want preaching to reflect their lives and encourage them in their struggles.
- *Relevant Preaching Connects Emotionally*: Postmoderns like the scriptures to come alive to the point where they can feel it.
- *Relevant Preaching Involves the Listener*: Postmoderns like to feel involved in what is being said.
- *Relevant Preaching is Authentic*: Postmoderns want their preachers to be "whole" people.
- *Preach from the Scriptures*: Postmoderns want the real thing. They want the scriptures, not some preacher's essay on life.
- *Preach Holistically*: Postmoderns do not want their faith compartmentalized. They are holistic people who want to have a holistic faith.[4]

A similar perspective on preaching to postmoderns is expressed by Graham Johnston in his book, *Preaching to a Postmodern World*. Johnston likens preaching today to the work of foreign missionaries. "Biblical communication to a postmodern culture should be approached in the same way that a missionary goes into a foreign culture. No missionary worth his or her salt would enter a field without first doing an exhaustive study of the culture he or she seeks to reach. The time has come for today's preachers to don the missionary garb."[5] Johnston goes on to write, "Many pastors would be surprised at how postmodern some long-standing members seem. Postmodern thinking creeps into our lives not necessarily through conscious choice but through a steady stream of bombardment via movies, magazines, song, and television. Our congregations gather each Sunday and nod at the appropriate spots in the sermon, but in their hearts many parishioners hold deep-seated beliefs and values more in keeping with a postmodern worldview than with a biblical one."[6] He sums up the preaching challenge for pastors today in the following way: "The task is to engage people anew, with a fresh voice so that even in this millennium, the gospel will remain the good news rather than yesterday's news. In the process, postmodernity will beg the question: 'Will we as preachers be known for being lovers of the truth or lovers of people?'"[7]

The challenge of preaching today with impact is even more complex in the intergenerational church. While most Gen Xers and Millennials would consider themselves to be postmoderns, a significant number of Boomers also embrace a postmodern worldview. At the same time, most Silents and GIs still have their feet and minds firmly rooted in the modern world. Consequently, trying to communicate with these different generations in the same sermon and worship service is a daunting task. This difficulty only highlights the fact that the Saturday and/or Sunday worship times play only a small part in the life of an effective intergenerational church. While sermons can be given with variety and effect to reach the different generations, the greatest impact of the intergenerational church is felt through 24/7 relationship building between the generations that will often take place on other days, in other ways, and in other venues.

In order to reach multiple generations in one sermon, preachers must understand what each generation expects from a sermon and what kind of communication they normally learn from and respond to. For example, the life experiences of both Gen Xers and Millennials have been saturated with technology. One of the major ways, if not *the* major way, these two generations get information is through technological sources like the Internet, e-mail, text messages, blogs, Twitter, YouTube, MP3 players, podcasts, DVDs, television, movies, etc. In communicating to Gen Xers and Millennials the use of multimedia productions can be helpful. Visual and sensory learning not only is their style, but technology also helps lengthen normally short attention spans. The use of pop cultural metaphors also can be useful in communicating biblical truths to these generations. Both Gen Xers and Millennials relate more to present illustrations than they do to historical references. In addition, sermon messages should embrace the multicultural, multiethnic, and global realities that match the world of Gen Xers and Millennials.

The length of sermons also needs to be reassessed. Many preachers believe they need to speak 30 minutes or more to get their message across. Today, most people from all the generations have difficulty paying attention for this length of time. A busy, chaotic world often invades the heads of most sermon listeners. While it is often more difficult to communicate succinctly, sermons will be more effective if deliverers use fewer words and use them more compellingly. Also, interspersing sermons with movie, music, or drama illustrations can add to communication effectiveness. Storytelling, either from the pastor or from congregation members, can also be a helpful way of providing insight and instruction. Whatever techniques or methodology used, the point is that when communicating biblical truth and application to a mixed modern/postmodern audience, much creativity is necessary.

To further complicate the communication process, Boomers may hold many of the same perspectives of the previous and following generations. That is, most Boomers can easily embrace a mix of modern and postmodern worldviews. When it comes to the use of technology and pop culture in sermons, Boomers will usually respond more to illustrations from TV, movies, and music rather than to illustrations from a digital world, such as video games, YouTube, or the Internet. And for Boomers, relationships are the most important subject that can be expressed in a sermon—with Jesus Christ, with family and friends, with our world. The importance of relationships is quite consistent among most members of the Boomer Generation. A relational pastor for Boomers is one that is likable, tolerant, and affirming as opposed to one that is stern, dogmatic, and authoritarian.

Boomers have often been described as "a generation of seekers." Boomer leaders and Boomer congregations have given us seeker services and the seeker-oriented church. One of the major misconceptions of the seeker movement has been that many new Boomer attendees who come to these churches are unchurched. The reality for most of these Boomers is that they are actually "rechurched." That is, most of the Boomers who attend a seeker-oriented church either never left organized religion or have been "church-broken" in other denominational churches. Megachurches swelled with Boomers during the 1970s, 1980s, and 1990s who returned to church primarily for the sake of their children. Much writing and discussion contends that this period in American church life was and is a time of "Christianity lite." As they become empty nesters, it remains to be seen whether churches will be able to hold Boomers. In fact, it now appears that many Boomers, as they become empty nesters, are growing increasingly bored with local churches. As young adults, many Boomers saw themselves as able to "change the world." Today, many Boomers still see themselves as world-changers. To reach them, pastors and sermons must cast a vision as big as the kingdom of God and engage Boomers in that vision.

Silents' and GIs' expectations for sermons are usually quite different. People in these generations who hold a predominately modern worldview will expect logical, well-thought-through sermons that have specific applications to their lives. Members of the GI and Silent Generation are generally linear, left-brain thinkers who respond well to a propositional approach and an expository style. GIs and Silents want the pastor to be an expert, or at least educated, on the ways of a faith journey. While these generations may accept transparency and authenticity from their ministers, it can make them somewhat uncomfortable. GIs and Silents are generally not at ease with the display of public emotion. They also hold a well-developed appreciation for institutional propriety. That is, GIs and Silents are more comfortable when church is done properly and in order.

While the task of preaching to an intergenerational congregation is challenging, it is still feasible. A few basic ground rules are necessary:

- Be authentic and communicate a message that is genuine. Do not try to manipulate a response—the congregation will easily see through it.
- Talk on topics and issues with which your congregation members are wrestling. Make sermons speak to real life, not theological theory.
- Always give practical ways of applying the message to their lives. Today's churchgoers want to see realistic ways that faith makes a difference 24/7.
- When possible and appropriate, use illustrations and examples from current events and pop culture. (Churchgoers lives are saturated with news events, TV programs, movies, music, and other media-driven information.) Use multimedia and various creative forms of communication to connect with the congregation. People today have relatively short attention spans and are used to variety and options—whether pastors like it or not.
- As often as possible, the sermon should relate to the everyday context of each of the generations in the congregation. That is, how does the message relate to high school students? What is the message to the young adult who

is trying to establish a stable adult lifestyle? How does the sermon relate to the Boomer who is looking for a life of significance? What is the application for the retiree who wants to know how to live out the days he or she has left? While it may not be possible to apply every sermon to every generation, it should be a goal.

- On regular occasions involve the congregation in the sermon. For example, ask questions that they will have to think through and answer on the spot—either to themselves or to the congregation. Allow for a time of silent or public prayer as a response to the sermon. Still yet, challenge the congregation to apply a response to the sermon during the week that could be reported on at the next worship service. The point is, be creative in the way a sermon is communicated and applied.

- Provide opportunities for various generations to interact around the sermon. For example, challenge families to discuss and apply the message. Get intergenerational groups to apply the sermon content through service and outreach. Again, thoughtful creativity is important.

- Finally, pastors should seek regular input from all the generations. The best sermons can come from pastors who have significant relationships with members of all the church's generations. Effective preaching will come when pastors understand the world of each of the generations to which he or she is trying to communicate.

Chapter 13
Intergenerational Teaching

When it comes to intergenerational teaching, many of the same perspectives on preaching are applicable. Still, intergenerational teaching has some additional considerations. As we have seen, different generations learn differently. The GI and Silent Generations are the last generations that will sit in a classroom-type setting and listen to a lecturer. Most members of these two generations still desire a traditional Sunday school class, and the teacher better know what he or she is talking about. Both GIs and Silents desire content and are more interested in substance than style or process. Classes that present topical material or Bible study generally work well with these two generations.

For Boomers, learning comes best through relational interaction or experience. That is, Boomers want to be directly involved in the learning process because they believe they have something important to contribute. Boomers have difficulty listening very long to a talking head. (Perhaps this is the influence of TV and the remote control.) Even the layout of the room is important to Boomers. Instead of classroom style seating, Boomers like circles where they can see everyone else and relate to them. The relational process is very important to the learning style of most Boomers.

As noted previously, Gen Xers, if they are in church at all, learn primarily through participation. Gen Xers have an even shorter attention span than Boomers and need activity. They will not sit and listen in any situation that they deem of little value. Many Gen Xers simply get up and leave. Like the Boomers, Gen Xers want to be actively involved in the learning process either through interaction or hands-on learning. Much of the spiritual learning Gen Xers experience does not take place in the church. It may be in a Starbucks talking to friends and others, or in a chat session, or through a blog on the Internet. Because Gen Xers generally do not relate well to structured learning situations, one-on-one mentoring can be an effective teaching and learning experience. Still yet, Gen Xers learn valuable spiritual lessons while traveling in other countries, living in other cultures, and relating to other people. Members of Generation X generally see the whole world as their classroom and are not going to limit their learning experiences to structured educational events.

The learning style and experiences of most Millennials seems to be a combination of all the previous generations. While Millennials are more tolerant of traditional classroom learning than Gen Xers, they also receive much of their learning through experience and technology. In addition, Millennials are a generation that has been nurtured on community service; giving back through community service projects has been built into the learning experiences of most Millennials. Churches can build on these experiences by using service, mission, and outreach events as learning tools that produce teachable moments.

As with all aspects of the intergenerational church, creativity and innovation should be valued highly when it comes to teaching and learning. The following are suggestions on intergenerational teaching that may stimulate creative thought and discussion:

- Develop an intergenerational mentoring program. Mentoring needs to be seen as a trend and not a fad. When establishing mentoring relationships it is important to understand that certain generations relate better to each other than others. Generally speaking, Gen Xers relate best to GIs and Silents; Millennials relate best to Boomers. One important consideration: many Gen Xers and Millennials desire mentors, but generally will not initiate the relationships. Boomers, Silents, and GIs must take the first step in beginning a mentoring relationship. Also, realize that "reverse mentoring," where older and younger generations learn from each other, is an important process to promote. (In recent years, much has been written about mentoring. Many resources are available on how best to develop a mentoring program in your church that will meet the needs of your people.)
- Establish intergenerational classes on topics of interest to all generations. Address topics such as "What is the value of pop culture?"; "Has technology made our lives better or worse?"; "How can we know truth?"; "How

can we find our purpose in life?"; "What does a healthy spiritual life look like?"; and other inclusive themes.

- Assist parents and grandparents to be the major moral and spiritual teachers in the lives of children and youth. For example, establish father-son and mother-daughter "rite of passage" classes and experiences.
- Adopt a philosophy of ministry that makes the home the center of spiritual growth and formation. To this end, provide parents with cross-generational materials, such as books and videos that allow all generations to learn from each other.
- Establish intergenerational teams to lead children's classes and other learning experiences, so as to provide children with regular interaction with members of all other generations.
- Provide venues and opportunities for older adults to tell their life stories to younger generations and vice versa. Many younger people are fascinated about the way the world used to be, while older adults need to hear what is like to come of age in today's world. Question and answer interchange will provide insights to all the generations about how times have changed and how they are the same.
- Revisit retirement and discuss alternatives to traditional thinking on retirement. Have Silent Generation retirees share the upsides and downsides of retirement with members of the Boomer Generation.

- Create if-I-had-to-do-it-over-again sessions where older adults can pass learned wisdom on to younger people.
- An intergenerational film festival or art and music weekend can bring multiple generations together to discuss how pop culture, art, and music impact their lives and their journeys of faith. Pop culture is especially important to the younger generations, yet many churches and church members have been fighting the culture wars for several decades. Instead, churches need dialogue across generations on how followers of Jesus Christ can redeem our culture while loving and serving others in his name.

Chapter 14
Intergenerational Community

While there is much talk about community among Christians, there is relatively little being experienced. Since the word *community* is often ill defined, there is much confusion, frustration, and futility in trying to establish it. In its basic form, community or "common unity" in the local church is realized when people share their lives in various ways as they follow Jesus Christ together. The church, as the interdependent body of Christ, is God's definition of community. In Acts 2:41-47, the early church gave us examples of how the church community behaved:

> Those who accepted his message were baptized, and about three thousand were added to their number that day. They devoted themselves to the apostles' teaching and to the fellowship, to the breaking of bread and to prayer. Everyone was filled with awe, and many wonders and miraculous signs were done by the apostles.
> All the believers were together and had everything in common. Selling their possessions and goods, they gave to anyone as he had need. Every day they continued to meet together in the temple courts. They broke bread in their homes and ate together

Peter Menconi

> with glad and sincere hearts, praising God and
> enjoying the favor of all the people. And the Lord
> added to their number daily those who were being
> saved.

While this account is more descriptive than prescriptive, it nonetheless gives us insight into how believers in a local church can relate to one another.

The most compelling message for us in this passage is that the followers of Jesus shared their lives. Sharing our lives with other believers in our individualistic society is a somewhat foreign concept, and yet we repeatedly see interdependence taught in the Bible. In 1 Corinthians 12 we read about the church:

> All these are the work of one and the same Spirit,
> and he gives them to each one, just as he determines. The body is a unit, though it is made up of
> many parts; and though all its parts are many, they
> form one body. So it is with Christ. For we were all
> baptized by one Spirit into one body—whether
> Jews or Greeks, slave or free—and we were all given
> the one Spirit to drink. Now the body is not made up
> of one part but of many. If the foot should say, "Because I am not a hand, I do not belong to the body,"
> it would not for that reason cease to be part of the
> body. And if the ear should say, "Because I am not
> an eye, I do not belong to the body," it would not
> for that reason cease to be part of the body. If the
> whole body were an eye, where would the sense of
> hearing be? If the whole body were an ear, where
> would the sense of smell be? But in fact God has
> arranged the parts in the body, every one of them,

just as he wanted them to be. If they were all one part, where would the body be? As it is, there are many parts, but one body.

While this level of interdependence is not natural for us, it is the foundation of a healthy local church, especially a healthy *intergenerational* church.

With a closer look at the above passages, we can glean some important characteristics of a vital Christian community. First, a commitment to following Jesus Christ is central to the vitality and strength of a body of believers. Second, the regular practices of teaching and learning, corporate prayer, taking meals together, and fellowship underscore that our journey with Jesus is not solitary. Third, our first century brothers and sisters were generous in meeting practical needs within the church, such as providing food and finances. We are to do the same. There are other lessons and characteristics that can be lifted from these passages and they can be used as a basis for an intergenerational discussion about the local church.

Another biblical passage that is foundational in understanding the intergenerational church is Romans 12. In verses 4-8 we read:

Just as each of us has one body with many members, and these members do not all have the same function, so in Christ we who are many form one body, and each member belongs to all the others. We have different gifts, according to the grace given us. If a man's gift is prophesying, let him use it in proportion to his faith. If it is serving, let him serve; if it is teaching, let him teach; if it is encouraging, let

> him encourage; if it is contributing to the needs of others, let him give generously; if it is leadership, let him govern diligently; if it is showing mercy, let him do it cheerfully.

Not only does this passage reiterate the intent of interdependence within the church—the body of Christ—but it also reminds us that *all* members of the body have gifts, abilities, and skills to offer in service to God.

The chapter goes on to describe what the behavior of believers should look like. In verses 9-21, the apostle Paul gives us instruction and direction that could easily occupy us for the rest of our days:

> Love must be sincere. Hate what is evil; cling to what is good. Be devoted to one another in brotherly love. Honor one another above yourselves. Never be lacking in zeal, but keep your spiritual fervor, serving the Lord. Be joyful in hope, patient in affliction, faithful in prayer. Share with God's people who are in need. Practice hospitality. Bless those who persecute you; bless and do not curse. Rejoice with those who rejoice; mourn with those who mourn. Live in harmony with one another. Do not be proud, but be willing to associate with people of low position. Do not be conceited. Do not repay anyone evil for evil. Be careful to do what is right in the eyes of everybody. If it is possible, as far as it depends on you, live at peace with everyone. Do not take revenge, my friends, but leave room for God's wrath, for it is written: "It is mine to avenge; I will repay," says the Lord. On the contrary: "If your enemy is hungry, feed him; if he is thirsty, give him something to drink. In

doing this, you will heap burning coals on his head."
Do not be overcome by evil, but overcome evil with
good.

These verses could be the rally call of the intergenerational church. For a local church to be truly intergenerational, each generation must honor one another above
themselves. Tolerance of one another will not get it done.
All members of the church must learn to genuinely appreciate people in the body who are different than themselves.
Simply put, as brothers and sisters in God's family, we are
on this journey together...*and we are better together.*

With this biblical foundation, a local church can begin to build an intergenerational community in numerous
ways. As in other areas of church life, creativity and innovation are quite helpful. The following suggestions on moving toward intergenerational community may be helpful,
but each church will need to customize their approach to
fit their unique situation and culture:

- Integrate multiple generations into the worship service as often as possible. For example,
  have multiple generations represented on
  your worship team. Give people from different generations an opportunity to preach and
  teach regularly. Allow people from each generation opportunities to lead prayer or give
  announcements.
- Schedule regular multigenerational church
  events as a way of building intergenerational
  community. Create events that integrate all
  generations and whole households. For example, all generations like to eat, so multigen-

erational dinners often work well. Make the events fun and build in activities that promote and encourage intergenerational communication. These events can take place outside the church walls as well as within the church building.

- Schedule regular sporting events that engage multiple generations. Most people, especially men and boys, loosen up with sports, such as multigenerational softball or volleyball games. Such times present an excellent opportunity for individuals and generations to see each other differently.

- Encourage family members to eat at least one meal a day together. In our busyness we seldom stop long enough to communicate and relate over a meal.

- Take opportunities to include non-nuclear family members in your family activities. Thanksgiving and Christmas holidays are great times to invite widows, singles, and single-parent families to join your festivities.

- Churches can create "new households" within the church community by encouraging non-nuclear families to meet and relate regularly. These new households can include nuclear families, blended families, single-parent families, singles, and others. This is a great way to build unity within the local church while preventing the isolation of many who attend our churches regularly. These groups can be formed as part of a church's small group ministry.

- There are more than 4 million grandparents in the United States who are daily helping to raise their grandchildren. Churches can help to provide support and community for grandparents in these situations.
- As mentioned previously, churches should develop opportunities for multiple generations to tell stories about their lives and journeys of faith that can be shared during worship services, in classes, during mentoring times, or at intergenerational social events. Telling our stories is a great way to promote intergenerational communication, understanding, and relationship.
- Develop mentoring relationships between younger and older congregation members. These relationships can include an older couple mentoring a younger or newly married couple or experienced parents mentoring younger or new parents. Mentoring relationships often develop through "grandfriends," where older adults befriend younger adults and youth.
- Develop opportunities for people of various generations to share their interests and hobbies. Create multigenerational opportunities for those interested in biking, hiking, woodworking, quilt making, writing, singing, boating, golfing, skiing, cooking, acting, painting, gardening, and other common activities. Bringing people from the various generations together around common interests is a very effective way of building intergenerational community.

- Create opportunities for multiple generations to see movies or read specific books together. Regular opportunities to discuss movies and books can help increase intergenerational communication, understanding, and community.
- Establish opportunities for youth and young adults to be exposed to older members' workplaces. Help young people view real life situations through the window of careers and work situations that may be of interest to them. Career insight, advice, and guidance provided by older members of the congregation can help build intergenerational community and serve younger adults.
- Organize an art exhibit or arts and crafts weekend with an invitation to the broader community. Involve multiple generations in the planning and execution of such events.
- Organize regular intergenerational mission trips and outreach projects.
- Above all, be creative and plan intergenerational activities that fit your church's culture.

Chapter 15
Intergenerational Outreach and Service

There is a growing movement among churches to define themselves as "externally focused," meaning that they look and serve outside the walls of the local church. In their book *The Externally Focused Church*, Rick Rusaw and Eric Swanson give four characteristics of such churches:

1. Externally focused churches are convinced that good deeds and good news can't and shouldn't be separated.
2. Externally focused churches see themselves as vital to the health and well being of their community.
3. Externally focused churches believe that ministering and serving are the normal expressions of Christian living.
4. Externally focused churches are evangelistically effective.[1]

One of the best ways for multiple generations within a church to develop relationships is by becoming externally focused and serving together. When the various generations corporately serve others, the focus is off generational differences and on working and cooperating together.

Peter Menconi

Through service, generations can readily learn from each other and learn to appreciate each other while growing in their relationship with Jesus Christ. The following are just a few ways that the various generations can serve others inside and outside the church:

- Members of Gen X and the Millennial Generation have experience helping others through community service, as it was and is part of their school curriculum. Churches can build on these experiences by offering multiple intergenerational occasions for service. Most communities have numerous opportunities to serve the poor and needy members of our cities and towns. Mercy ministries afford chances for intergenerational groups to serve in food pantries and soup kitchens, while food and clothes collection and distribution are other common ways of serving. More sophisticated ministry opportunities for cross-generational service also exist such as helping construct affordable housing with organizations like Habitat for Humanity. Many cities have urban gardens. Multiple generations from a suburban church can partner and serve together with multiple generations from an urban church growing food and distributing it to poor families and individuals.

- Start businesses that help the unemployed and underemployed find rewarding jobs. Business as ministry is an underutilized vehicle for outreach and service. Active and retired businesspersons can work with youth and young adults in providing jobs and income while teaching business skills and providing on-the-job training. Creative micro-enterprise ventures, such as those that manufacture needed items, can bring generations together both from inside and outside the local church.

- Take intergenerational short-term mission trips together. Make these mission trips a regular part of your church's outreach ministry. Short-term mission trips are one of the quickest ways to build solid, long-lasting relationships between generations. When an intergenerational group is together in a neutral—and often uncomfortable environment—conversations are more easily initiated. Mission trips afford wonderful teachable moments for adults, youth, and children. Debrief these trips together and discuss ways your short-term trips can have long-term impact.
- Brainstorm and develop creative ways to minister to homebound seniors and nursing home residents. Young children and older adults often bond quickly.
- Create intergenerational teams that can minister to the elderly and single-parent families through home repairs, yard work, and other hands-on ways of serving.
- Create events or piggyback on opportunities to improve the environment through tree planting, picking up trash along roadways or trails, improving hiking trails, or other "green" initiatives. The outdoors provides a neutral environment for different generations to interact.

- Offer creative venues for retirees to use their gifts, talents, education, and experiences in ministry to children and youth both inside and outside the church. Tutoring and mentoring programs can connect active and caring older adults with at-risk children, for example. These relationships can focus on improving reading, math, or computer skills. More and more local schools are looking for older adults to tutor and mentor students. Another connection between generations can come through teaching and learning the arts. Still another venue for intergenerational contact is afforded through work with special needs children. The possibilities are limited only by our creativity and vision.

- Since becoming a parent for the first time is usually a stressful experience, create opportunities for experienced mothers and fathers to support and assist first-time parents.

- Create teams of people who can offer a "parent's night out" for parents of preschool and elementary-aged children. These teams can be made up of middle and high school youth, singles, parents with older children, and empty nesters. Church nurseries and other facilities can be used as centralized childcare venues. Such events also help build intergenerational community among the various generations providing childcare.

- Most cities and towns have many parachurch ministries that meet needs in a variety of ways. Consequently, it is not usually necessary to create your own opportunities for outreach and service. Partner with these ministries to involve your people in serving others. It may be necessary for your church's leadership to explore and investigate these opportunities and to decide on those that best fit your congregation.

- Intergenerational outreach and service opportunities can be experienced through the development of a sister church relationship with a church in a different community. For example, an Anglo church in the suburbs and an ethnic church in the city may want to start a ministry partnership. An urban/suburban ministry partnership can broaden the perspectives of both churches and make them more effective in ministering to their communities. In addition, when building relationships between the churches, each congregation will learn to appreciate each other while crossing ethnic, racial, generational, educational, socioeconomic and other traditional barriers. Remember, we are the body of Christ—*we are better together.*

- If people from your congregation are ministering overseas, create intergenerational home-front teams that will support them in a variety of ways. Encouragement and support can come in the form of regular e-mail correspondence, special care packages, birthday cards, financial help during emergencies, prayer, and through numerous other anticipated and unanticipated ways. Consider the possibility of this home-front team visiting your overseas ministry partners.

Peter Menconi

- Since the younger generations see the world as their backyard, consider recruiting them for intergenerational "vision trips" to educate the congregation on the needs around the world. New ministry initiatives may grow out of trips designed for exploration and fact finding.

Chapter 16
The Intergenerational Challenge

If everyone in the church easily found their place and did their part to make church ministry successful, this book would not be necessary. But that is not the way it works. Church ministry is, in fact, a messy endeavor that can be one of the most challenging anyone can undertake. Unlike business in which paychecks can be leveraged to get the desired responses and behavior, the church is predominantly a volunteer organization with different motives and motivations. The primary motivation should come from one's desire to follow Jesus Christ. Scripture repeatedly reminds us that the church is the body of Christ with Jesus as the head. And the local church is just one small part of a much bigger whole and much bigger reality: the kingdom of God. Without a kingdom perspective, a local church runs the risk of becoming a mutual admiration society. Simply put, the church is not about us—not the pastor, not you, not the congregation, not the denomination. Ephesians 4:15 tells us that instead of focusing on ourselves "we will in all things grow up into him who is the Head, that is, Christ."

The major role of church leaders is to help members of the congregation take the next step in their journey with Jesus, perhaps one of the first for a new follower or one of the last for those who have followed Christ for many years. Helping congregation members find their calling is a key role for church leadership. Just as the apostle Paul urged Timothy "to fan into flame the gift of God" that he had been given, so pastors and church leaders are to fan the flame that God has put in the hearts of each of his children. The challenges of an intergenerational church will be met only when church leaders learn how to advance people along their ever-maturing journey with Jesus. Additionally, leadership will need to pass this ministry skill on to others within the congregation as the body builds the body.

The challenges of the intergenerational church are also best met when we understand the unique needs of each generation and think creatively on how these needs can be met. When we address needs within a congregation, we not only are dealing with what people will receive, but we also are addressing what people need in order to serve and give. Most people in our local churches want their lives to count for something and leaders need to be able to make this happen. To this end, let's look at the specific needs of each of the church's generations.

The GI Challenge

With each passing day, more and more members of the GI Generation are leaving us. Yet for the ones who remain, there are real needs that local churches can address. While many GIs are in nursing homes and extended-care facilities, many others remain in their homes and apartments. With decreasing mobility, many GIs find themselves attending church services less frequently. Providing recordings of worship services helps keep some of them connected to the congregation. Other obvious opportunities to minister to GIs come through providing transportation to church, shopping, doctor's appointments, and elsewhere. In addition, visitation to senior housing facilities, nursing homes, and extended-care facilities by younger people is very welcomed and appreciated.

But not all GIs are care receivers. Many members of the GI Generation are still able to minister to others. Churches can give vital GIs the opportunity to act as surrogate grandparents to families who are separated (either geographically or through estrangement) from their biological relatives. Additionally, younger generations should hear the life stories of GIs before they are all gone. They have lived through a unique period of American history and have seen incredible changes in their lifetimes. All younger generations can benefit from hearing GIs' life histories. Local churches can provide opportunities for these stories to be heard, recorded, and handed down. This transference of wisdom and perspective is especially important since American culture is so devoid of true sages.

The Silent Challenge

Like every other generation, members of the Silent Generation offer a unique challenge to local churches. Since the leadership reins of many churches are in the hands of Silents, tension abounds between them and the younger generations. Most of this tension results from a profoundly different way of looking at the world. As noted previously, most Silents have their feet firmly rooted in the modern world. The younger generations are much more influenced by a postmodern approach to life. Consequently, there is often profound disagreement on how church should be done. A major challenge for local churches will be to help members of the Silent Generation accept and integrate some of the worldview of younger generations. Unfortunately, many Silent leaders too often do not see the value of change, entrenching themselves in a business-as-usual mindset.

When addressing the needs of the Silent generation, local churches must understand the significance of their current life situation. Most Silents are currently retired and many are looking for significant ways to invest their lives. If churches do not learn to engage Silents in significant and meaningful ministry opportunities, they may lose them to sunbelt retirement communities. Younger leadership must respect and incorporate Silents into church life, as they have much to offer. At the same time, church leaders from the Silent Generation must show patience with younger generations and not run them off with their intransigent leadership. To reiterate, we are better together, but we need to work at it.

The Boomer Challenge

The Boomer Generation offers the greatest hope for the establishment of intergenerational churches. As the central generation, they can look both to the past and the future. Old enough to have learned from the school of hard knocks and young enough to still be idealistic and forward looking, Boomers possess the potential to bridge the gap between the generations before them and those that have come after them. But building these bridges will not be easy. As noted earlier, Silents do not especially like the style and attitude of Boomers, yet many will readily follow Boomers' lead in the church—if it makes sense. Gen Xers also do not readily take to Boomers, unless they find them to be genuine, real, and authentic. Boomers must first win Gen Xers' trust. There will probably be relatively little tension between Boomers and Millennials, but this remains to be seen.

While the main challenge of forming successful intergenerational churches may fall to Boomers, all other generations need to be involved as well. Boomer leadership should be very knowledgeable about and sensitive to other generational members' viewpoints. With their emphasis on relationships, Boomers need to initiate healthy interaction between all the generations. They must create multiple venues and opportunities that will allow members of all generations to worship together, serve together, play together, grow together, and simply be together. Because of their tendency to be the center of attention, Boomers must take care not to dominate, but instead to listen, facilitate, and integrate. While the task of developing an intergenerational church may seem daunting, it is well worth the effort.

The Gen X Challenge

Since Generation X is the least represented in our local churches today, getting them to return and participate is a major challenge. If Gen Xers are to engage or re-engage in local churches, it must be through relationships. Gen Xers will respond to the establishment of genuine and authentic relationships among their peers and with members of the other generations. Generally speaking, Gen Xers respond better to GIs and Silents than they do to Boomers. Local churches have the challenge and opportunity to creatively establish relationships with Gen Xers through mentoring programs—with individuals, couples, new parents, and families. Gen Xers also will engage in service and mission projects that seek to help the poor, make the environment better, and generally make the world a better place.

Incorporating Gen Xers into leadership may be a major challenge for many local churches. Gen Xers are not usually joiners, but will involve themselves in leadership situations where they are accepted as peers, respected, and allowed to be creative. In fact, local churches need Gen Xers to fill leadership roles as they help interpret and navigate an increasingly postmodern culture.

The Millennial Challenge

Local churches face a major challenge ministering to and through Millennials because of their eclectic worldview. As noted earlier in the research from the National Study of Youth and Religion, most Millennials embrace religious beliefs that level the playing field, meaning Millennials' religious beliefs are so diluted that they encompass almost any way of living life. They basically believe that if you are a nice person, everything else will work out. This view, labeled Moralistic Therapeutic Deism, indicates that local churches need to better communicate the temporal and eternal truths given to us by God in the Bible. The pervasive belief among Millennials that being a follower of Jesus Christ is just one good option among many others is difficult to overcome. It remains to be seen whether this naïve and immature stance will continue as Millennials age.

As with Gen Xers, pastors and church leaders will need to learn new postmodern ways to communicate the timeless truths of the Gospel. Most of this postmodern communication will need to center on the person of Jesus Christ. To most people of all generations, Jesus Christ is an attractive person. To Boomers, Gen Xers, and Millennials, it will be more helpful for pastors and church leaders to talk about what it means to be a *follower of Jesus Christ* than it will be to talk about what it means to be a *Christian*. (Unfortunately, the term *Christian* today carries a myriad of negative connotations.)

Despite potential difficulties, the goal of establishing an intergenerational church offers many powerful opportunities. Through healthy intergenerational relationships, communication, and action, the church can offer an anguished world a more honest representation of our loving and just God. Churches that make room for all generations will not only be attractive to believers, but they will also be noticed by nonbelievers. Healthy intergenerational communication and community is so rare in our culture that a church that succeeds at both will become like a city on a hill. It will exude light, impart power, radiate warmth, and invite strangers. Its influence will shine far beyond its walls.

All of us, from every generation who are God's children, have been given his mission. God's mission is to redeem his broken creation. That's why the Father sent the Son; the Father and Son sent the Spirit; and the Father, Son, and Spirit send us, the church, into the world to carry on his mission of redemption. The work of redemption has no age requirement; we are to be about God's work together; and we can do it better together. As we endeavor to carry out

God's mission together, let us allow the words of Jesus to resonate in our ears and penetrate our hearts, "You are the light of the world. A city on a hill cannot be hidden. Neither do people light a lamp and put it under a bowl. Instead they put it on its stand, and it gives light to everyone in the house. In the same way, let your light shine before men, that they may see your good deeds and praise your Father in heaven."

The Intergenerational Matrix

The following matrix will summarize some of the major differences between the five generations in the church today. Pastors, church leaders and attendees can use it as a tool to begin the process of becoming a truly intergenerational church. The exercises that follow will also assist leaders in moving toward this important goal.

The Intergenerational Church

	GI Generation	Silent Generation	Boomer Generation	Generation X	Millennial Generation
Worship Style	Formal/ traditional	Traditional/ predictable	Informal	Eclectic/artistic/ informal	Eclectic/ informal
Worship Music	Traditional hymns	Traditional hymns/ choruses	Contemporary choruses	New emergent songs	Some of all types of music
Preaching/ Teaching	Practical	Professional	Relational	Interactive	Integrated
Community	Family-based	Collegial	Networks of relationships	Tribes	Global
Leadership Style	Chain of command	Corporate/ committees	Team	Individualistic	"Three-dimensional"
Theology/ Faith	Private	Propositional	Practical	Contextual	Global
View of God	Distant father	Creator and truth giver	Friend and ally	Compassionate healer	Global connector
Worldview	God is in control of the world	The laws of the universe are at work	The physical, emotional and spiritual worlds are all interrelated	The world is chaotic and broken	The world can be "fixed"
Values	Family/ country/ security	Truth/ education/ security	Tolerance/ money/time	Genuineness/ acceptance/fun	Competence/ options
Work Ethic	"Do whatever it takes"	Loyalty/ stable work/ longevity	Work hard/ play hard/ meaningful work	Work to play/ frequent job changes	Work as a "video game"
Relationships	More formal and positional	Congenial and sense of propriety	Informal and competitive	Individualistic and tribal	Friendships within groups
Needs	Acceptance/ companion-ship	Inclusion/ stability in midst of chaos	Sense of purpose and significance to "change the world"	Sense of belonging/hope/ opportunities to "heal"/mentors	Intergenerational acceptance and understanding/ mentors

Chapter 1—Worksheet
Why Intergenerational Ministry?

Use this worksheet to begin the process of becoming an intergenerational church. As you work through these initial exercises and questions, you will quickly know how open your church leadership is to including all generations in the life and ministry of your church.

1. With your church leaders, do a study on what the Bible has to say about generations. Read the following passages and discuss the questions that follow: (all passages from NIV).

Genesis 17:5-7

> 5   *No longer will you be called Abram; your name will be Abraham, for I have made you a father of many nations.*
> 6   *I will make you very fruitful; I will make nations of you, and kings will come from you.*
> 7   *I will establish my covenant as an everlasting covenant between me and you and your descendants after you for the generations to come, to be your God and the God of your descendants after you.*

Peter Menconi

Exodus 12:13-14

13   *The blood will be a sign for you on the houses where you are; and when I see the blood, I will pass over you. No destructive plague will touch you when I strike Egypt.*

14   *This is a day you are to commemorate; for the generations to come you shall celebrate it as a festival to the LORD—a lasting ordinance.*

Deuteronomy 7:9

8   *Know therefore that the LORD your God is God; he is the faithful God, keeping his covenant of love to a thousand generations of those who love him and keep his commands.*

Deuteronomy 32:7

1   *Remember the days of old; consider the generations long past. Ask your father and he will tell you, your elders, and they will explain to you.*

Job 8:8-9

8   *Ask the former generations and find out what their fathers learned,*

9   *for we were born only yesterday and know nothing, and our days on earth are but a shadow.*

Psalms 22:30-31

> 30 *Posterity will serve him; future generations will be told about the Lord.*
> 31 *They will proclaim his righteousness to a people yet unborn—for he has done it.*

Ephesians 3:20-21

> 20 *Now to him who is able to do immeasurably more than all we ask or imagine, according to his power that is at work within us,*
> 21 *to him be glory in the church and in Christ Jesus throughout all generations, for ever and ever! Amen.*

a. How important do you think generations are to God? Why did you answer as you did?

b. In what ways can we as children of God relate to the generations that have come before us?

c. How are we to view the generations of believers that have preceded us?

d. What are our responsibilities to the generations that follow us?

Peter Menconi

2. With your leadership group, scan a good concordance and observe how many times the Bible refers to *generations*.

    a.   Discuss why your leaders should pay more attention to the different generations in your church.

    b.   Have each leader share how important they believe it is for your church to become more intergenerational.

    c.   Determine which of your church leaders are committed to continuing the process of becoming more intentionally intergenerational.

Know Your Church: Who are You, Really?

The primary purpose of this worksheet is to help your church leadership learn who your congregation really is. The following sample survey can help your church leadership begin to understand the generational makeup and needs of your congregation.

Sample Congregational Survey

The leadership of our church desires to see our body minister and be ministered to as effectively as possible. But we need your help in shaping the future of our church. In order to understand the assets and needs of our congregation we are asking you to prayerfully complete the following survey. You do not have to sign your name to this survey. All responses received will be kept in confidence. Please return the survey to _____ by_____.

Please either circle your response or fill in the blank. Thank you!

1. To which of our generations do you belong?
   a. GI Generation (born 1906-1924)
   b. Silent Generation (born 1925-1943)

    c.   Boomer Generation (born 1944-62)

    d.   Generation X (born 1963-81)

    e.   Millennial Generation (born 1982-2000)

2.   How far do you travel to attend our church?

    a.   Under 2 miles

    b.   2-5 miles

    c.   5-10 miles

    d.   More than 10 miles

3.   Which of the following statements best describes why you attend this church?

    a.   "I've attended church all my life—it's a habit."

    b.   "I want to know God better."

    c.   "I come to worship God."

    d.   "I want to meet other people."

    e.   "I desire to learn what the Bible says."

    f.   "I'm curious about God's will for my life."

    g.   "I would like to serve God and others."

    h.   "I'm looking for answers to my problems."

    i.   "I come because I'm desperate."

    j.   "I want to find a mate."

    k.   "I desire to expose my kids to moral and ethical teachings."

    l.   "I want to get into heaven."

    m.   "I come because my friends are here."

    n.   "I am looking to grow spiritually."

    o.   "I want to help change the world."

    p.   "I would like to find peace."

    q.   _____

4.   In what ministries are you or would you like to be involved?

    a.   Worship team
    b.   Music ministry
    c.   Children's ministry
    d.   Youth ministry
    e.   Small group ministry
    f.   Women's ministry
    g.   Men's ministry
    h.   Outreach ministry
    i.   Missions ministry
    j.   Prayer ministry
    k.   Caring ministry
    l.   _____

5.   In what ways is our church effective in ministering to your generation?

6.   In what ways can our church improve ministry to your generation?

7.   What suggestions do you have that will make ministry in and through our church more effective?

If you would like to talk to someone about this survey, please call_____ at_____ or we can contact you: Your phone # _____ or e-mail address _____

This survey is only a suggestion and a start. You will need to tailor your survey to meet the specific needs and concerns of your church.

Peter Menconi

The following are some questions your church leadership can use to stimulate discussion, make decisions, and move forward:

1. Are there any surprises in these survey results? If so, what are they?
2. Which generations are represented the most in your church? Which the least?
3. What are some of the reasons for these age groupings?
4. How does the generational breakdown of our church compare with the generational breakdown of our community? (Do you know the generational breakdown of your community? If not, some research is in order. Many demographic databases are available from your local government and other resources.)
5. Does our church leadership have any desire to change the generational makeup of our church? If not, why not? If so, why?
6. How might our church go about attracting larger numbers of poorly attending generations?

Chapter 3—Worksheet
The GI Generation

The goal of this worksheet is to help your church leaders and congregation better understand and minister to the GI Generation. It is best for the church leadership to first reflect on these questions individually and then to discuss them as a group. Remember, the goal is to become an effective intergenerational church and not simply to discuss differences in opinion and perspective.

1. Determine and discuss the GI Generation representation in your congregation. You can do this by answering the following questions:
    a. What percentage of your congregation is made up of members of the GI Generation?

    b. Are they fairly or disproportionately represented in your congregation and church leadership numbers?

    c. What impact do they have on your church? Are they primarily "givers" or "takers?"

2. What can the current church leadership learn from these GI Generation members and attendees?

3. What resources do GIs possess that can be included to make the church's ministry more effective?

4. Are there networks of relationships that the GIs possess that can help ministry effectiveness? If so, what are they?

5. What needs do your GIs have that are currently being met by the church's ministries? What needs are currently not being met?

Chapter 4—Worksheet
The Silent Generation

The goal of this worksheet is to help your church leaders and congregation better understand and minister to the Silent Generation. It is best for the church leadership to first reflect on these questions individually and then to discuss them as a group. Remember, the goal is to become an effective intergenerational church and not simply to discuss differences in opinion and perspective.

1. Determine and discuss the Silent Generation representation in your congregation. You can do this by answering the following questions:
   a. What percentage of your congregation is made up of members of the Silent Generation?

   b. Are they fairly or disproportionately represented in your congregation and church leadership numbers?

   c. What impact do they have on your church? Are they primarily "givers" or "takers?"

2. What can the current church leadership learn from these Silent Generation members and attendees?

Peter Menconi

3. What resources do Silents possess that can be included to make the church's ministry more effective?

4. Are there networks of relationships that the Silents possess that can help ministry effectiveness? If so, what are they?

5. What needs do your Silents have that are currently being met by the church's ministries? What needs are currently not being met?

The Boomer Generation

The goal of this worksheet is to help your church leaders and congregation better understand and minister to the Boomer Generation. It is best for the church leadership to first reflect on these questions individually and then to discuss them as a group. Remember, the goal is to become an effective intergenerational church and not simply to discuss differences in opinion and perspective.

1. Determine and discuss the Boomer Generation representation in your congregation. You can do this by answering the following questions:

   a. What percentage of your congregation is made up of members of the Boomer Generation?

   b. Are they fairly or disproportionately represented in your congregation and church leadership numbers?

   c. What impact do they have on your church? Are they primarily "givers" or "takers?"

Peter Menconi

2. What can the current church leadership learn from these Boomer Generation members and attendees?

3. What resources do Boomers possess that can be included to make the church's ministry more effective?

4. Are there networks of relationships that the Boomers possess that can help ministry effectiveness? If so, what are they?

5. What needs do your Boomers have that are currently being met by the church's ministries? What needs are currently not being met?

Chapter 6—Worksheet
Generation X

The goal of this worksheet is to help your church leaders and congregation better understand and minister to Generation X. It is best for the church leadership to first reflect on these questions individually and then to discuss them as a group. Remember, the goal is to become an effective intergenerational church and not simply to discuss differences of opinion and perspective.

1. Determine and discuss the representation of Generation X in your congregation. You can do this by answering the following questions:
   a. What percentage of your congregation is made up of Gen Xers?

   b. Are they fairly or disproportionately represented in your congregation and church leadership numbers?

   c. What impact do they have on your church? Are they primarily "givers" or "takers?"

2. What can the current church leadership learn from these Generation X members and attendees?

3. What resources do Gen Xers possess that can be included to make the church's ministry more effective?

4. Are there networks of relationships that Gen Xers possess that can help ministry effectiveness? If so, what are they?

5. What needs do your Xers have that are currently being met by the church's ministries? What needs are currently not being met?

Chapter 7—Worksheet
The Millennial Generation

The goal of this worksheet is to help your church leaders and congregation better understand and minister to Millennials. It is best for the church leadership to first reflect on these questions individually and then to discuss them as a group. Remember, the goal is to become an effective intergenerational church and not simply to discuss differences in opinion and perspective.

1. Determine and discuss the representation of the Millennial Generation in your congregation. You can do this by answering the following questions:
   a. What percentage of your congregation is made up of Millennials?

   b. What is their impact on the congregation? Are they fairly or disproportionately represented in your congregation and church leadership numbers?

   c. What impact do they have on your church? Are they primarily "givers" or "takers?"

2. What can the current church leadership learn from these Millennial members and attendees?

3. What resources do Millennials possess that can be included to make the church's ministry more effective?

4. Are there networks of relationships that Millennials possess that can help ministry effectiveness? If so, what are they?

5. What needs do your Millennials have that are currently being met by the church's ministries? What needs are currently not being met?

Notes

Chapter 3

[1] *20th Century Day by Day: 100 Years of News from January 1, 1900 to December 31, 1999* (London: Dorling Kindersley, 2000), p. 360.

Chapter 4

[1] William H. Whyte, *The Organization Man* (New York: Doubleday-Anchor, 1956).

Chapter 5

[1] David Frum, *How We Got Here: The 70s- The Decade that Brought You Modern Life (For Better or Worse)* (New York: Basic Books, 2000), p. xxiii.

[2] Bruce Schulman, *The Seventies: The Great Shift in American Culture, Society, and Politics* (Cambridge, MA: Da Capo Press, 2002), p. 257.

[3] Wade Clark Roof, *Spiritual Marketplace: Baby Boomers and the Remaking of American Religion* (Princeton, New Jersey: Princeton University Press, 1999), p. 16.

Peter Menconi

[4]Wade Clark Roof, *A Generation of Seekers: The Spiritual Journeys of the Baby Boom Generation* (San Francisco: Harper Collins, 1993), p. 76.

Chapter 6

[1]Judith Wallerstein, Julia Lewis, and Sandra Blakeslee, *The Unexpected Legacy of Divorce: A 25 Year Landmark Study* (New York: Hyperion, 2000).

[2]Tom Beaudoin, *Virtual Faith: The Irreverent Spiritual Quest of Generation X* (San Francisco: Jossey-Bass Publishers, 1998), p. 5.

[3]*Time,* www.time.com/time/time100/.

[4]Mark I. Pinsky, *The Gospel According to The Simpsons: The Spiritual Life of the World's Most Animated Family* (Westminster: John Knox Press, 2001), p. 9.

[5]Matt Groening, *Mother Jones* interview (San Francisco: Mother Jones, March-April, 1999).

[6]Mark I. Pinsky, *The Gospel According to The Simpsons: The Spiritual Life of the World's Most Animated Family* (Westminster: John Knox Press, 2001), p. 42.

[7]Ibid., p. 51.

[8] J. Walker Smith and Ann Clurman, *Rocking the Ages: The Yankelovich Report on Generational Marketing* (New York: HarperBusiness, 1997).

[9] Kevin Graham Ford, *Jesus for a New Generation: Putting the Gospel in the Language of Xers* (Downers Grove, IL: InterVarsity Press, 1995), p. 154.

[10] William Mahedy and Janet Bernardi, *A Generation Alone: Xers Making a Place in the World* (Downers Grove, IL: InterVarsity Press, 1994), p. 28.

[11] Ibid., p. 80.

[12] *The State of Our Unions: The Social Health of Marriage in America* <http://marriage.rutgers.edu/publicat.htm>, 2001.

[13] Pamela Paul, *The Starter Marriage and the Future of Matrimony* (New York: Villard, 2002).

[14] Steve Rabey, *In Search of Authentic Faith: How Emerging Generations are Transforming the Church* (Colorado Springs: WaterBrook Press, 2001), p. 71.

[15] Scott M. Stanley, *The Power of Commitment: A Guide to Active, Lifelong Love* (San Francisco, CA: Jossey-Bass, 2005), p. 17.

[16] Rick and Kathy Hicks, *Boomers, Xers, and other Strangers* (Wheaton, IL: Tyndale House Publishers, 1999), p. 262.

Peter Menconi

[17]Bruce Tulgan, *Managing Generation X* (New York: W.W. Norton & Co., 2000), p. 46.

[18]Ibid., p. 170.

[19]Sarah E. Hinlicky, *First Things* (New York: February, 1999), p. 10-11.

[20]Ibid., p. 10-11.

[21]*Twentysomethings Struggle to Find Their Place in Christian Churches* (Ventura, CA: Barna Research Online, September 24, 2003), <www.barna.org>.

[22]Eddie Gibbs, *Church Next: Quantum Changes in How We Do Ministry* (Downers Grove, IL: InterVarsity Press, 2000), p. 123.

[23]Tom Beaudoin, *Virtual Faith: The Irreverent Spiritual Quest of Generation X* (San Francisco: Jossey-Bass Publishers, 1998), p. 26.

[24]LaTonya Taylor, "The Church of O," (Carol Stream, IL: *Christianity Today*, 4/1/02, Vol.46, No. 4).

[25]Ibid.

[26]*Barna Identifies Seven Paradoxes Regarding America's Faith* (Ventura,CA: Barna Research Online, December 17, 2002), <www.barna.org>.

[27]Ibid.

[28]Eddie Gibbs, *Church Next: Quantum Changes in How We Do Ministry* (Downers Grove, IL: InterVarsity Press, 2000), p. 128.

[29]Jimmy Long, *Generating Hope: A Strategy for Reaching the Postmodern Generation*, (Downers Grove, IL: InterVarsity Press, 1997), p. 83.

[30]Todd Hahn and David Verhaagen, *GenXers After God* (Grand Rapids, MI: Baker Books, 1998), p. 38.

Chapter 7

[1]Chap Clark, *Hurt: Inside the World of Today's Teenagers* (Grand Rapids, MI: Baker Publishing, 2004), p. 58.

[2]Neil Howe and William Strauss, "Through prism of tragedy, generations are defined," (Quoted in the September 23, 2002 edition of *The Christian Science Monitor*), <http://www.csmonitor.com/2002/0923/p09s01-coop.html>.

[3]*Time*, "Sport Crazed Kids" (July 12, 1999).

[4]Neil Howe and William Strauss, *Millennials Rising: The Next Great Generation* (New York: Vintage Books, 2000), p. 7.

[5]Ibid., p. 7-10.

Peter Menconi

[6]<www.pewinternet.org>.

[7]Ibid.

[8]"Generation 2001: A Survey of the First College Graduating Class of the New Millennium," <www.harrisinteractive.com>.

[9]Christian Smith and Melinda Lundquist Denton, *Soul Searching: The Religious and Spiritual Lives of American Teenagers* (New York, NY: Oxford University Press, 2005).

[10]Wendy Murray Zoba, *Generation 2K: What Parents and Others Need to Know About the Millennials* (Downers Grove, IL: InterVarsity Press, 1999), p. 64.

Chapter 8

[1]Jackson W. Carroll and Wade Clark Roof, *Bridging Divided Worlds: Generational Cultures in Congregations* (San Francisco: Jossey-Bass, 2002), p. 47.

[2]Ibid., p. 10-11.

[3]The Barna Group, "Twentysomethings Struggle to Find Their Place in Christian Churches" (Ventura, CA: The Barna Group, September, 24, 2003), <www.barna.org>.

[4]Charles and Win Arn, *The New Senior: Preparing Your Church for the Age Wave* (Pasadena, CA: Church Growth Press, 2002).

[5] Jimmy Carter, *The Virtues of Aging,* (New York: The Ballantine Publishing Group, 1998), p. 11.

Chapter 9

[1] Eddie Gibbs, *LeadershipNext: Changing Leaders in a Changing Culture* (Downers Grove, IL: InterVarsity Press, 2005), p. 86.

[2] Darrell L. Guder and others, *Missional Church: A Vision for the Sending of the Church in North America* (Grand Rapids, MI: Wm. B. Eerdmans Publishing Co., 1998), p. 11-12.

[3] Dan Kimball, *The Emerging Church* (Grand Rapids, MI: Zondervan, 2003), p. 95.

[4] Ed Stetzer and David Putnam, *Breaking the Missional Code: Your Church Can Become a Missionary in Your Community* (Nashville, TN: B&H Publishers, 2006), p. 48.

[5] Reggie McNeal, *The Present Future: Six Tough Questions for the Church* (San Francisco, CA: Jossey-Bass, 2003).

[6] George Barna, *Revolution: Finding Vibrant Faith Beyond the Walls of the Sanctuary* (Carol Stream, IL: Tyndale House Publishers, 2005), p. 42-47.

Peter Menconi

Chapter 10

[1]Andy Stanley, *The Next Generation Leader* (Sisters, Oregon: Multnomah Publishers, 2003), p. 11.

[2]Ibid., p. 11-12.

[3]Tim Conder, *The Church in Transition: The Journey of Existing Churches into the Emerging Culture* (Grand Rapids, MI: Zondervan, 2006), p. 133.

[4]Alan J. Roxburgh and Fred Romanuk, *The Missional Leader: Equipping Your Church to Reach a Changing World* (San Francisco, CA: Jossey-Bass, 2006), p. 125-141.

Chapter 11

[1]Robert E. Webber, *Planning Blended Worship: The Creative Mixture of Old and New* (Nashville: Abingdon Press, 1998), p. 29.

[2]Paul A. Basden, ed., *Exploring the Worship Spectrum* (Grand Rapids, MI: Zondervan, 2004), p. 11-12.

[3]Ibid., p. 12.

[4]Robert E. Webber, *Blended Worship: Achieving Substance and Relevance in Worship,* (Peabody, MA: Hendrickson Publishers, 1996), p. 51.

[5]Ibid., p. 66.

Chapter 12

[1]<www.faithworks.com/articles/articles2.htm>

[2]Ibid.

[3]Dave Teague, "Getting Started in Postmodern Preaching" <www.postmodernpreaching.net>

[4]Ibid.

[5]Graham Johnston, *Preaching to a Postmodern World* (Grand Rapids, MI: Baker Books, 2001), p. 10.

[6]Ibid., p. 15.

[7]Ibid., p. 20.

Chapter 14

[1]Rick Rusaw and Eric Swanson, *The Externally Focused Church* (Loveland, CO: Group Publishing, 2004).

About the Author

Born and raised in Chicago, Pete Menconi is a card-carrying member of Cub Fans Anonymous. He graduated from the University of Illinois, College of Dentistry and practiced dentistry for 22 years in private practice, the U.S. Army and at a mission hospital in Kenya, East Africa. In addition, Pete has a M.S. in Counseling Psychology and several years of seminary training. He has been a commodity futures floor trader, a speaker with the American Dental Society, and a broker of medical and dental practices. He has co-written a 9-book Bible study series and numerous articles and books.

For the past 19 years Pete has been the outreach pastor at Greenwood Community Church in suburban Denver, Colorado where he oversees the church's ministries from their doorstep to many places around the world.

Pete has been married to Jean for 41 years. They have three grown children and eight grandchildren.

Peter Menconi can be reached at petermenconi@msn.com.